Facing the Issues

Facing the Issues

Creative Strategies for
Probing Critical Social Concerns

Robert E. Myers

Zephyr Press
Tucson, Arizona

Facing the Issues
Creative Strategies for Probing Critical Social Concerns

Grades 6–12

©1994 by Zephyr Press
Printed in the United States of America

ISBN 1-56976-009-8

Editors: Stacey Lynn and Stacey Shropshire
Cover design: David Fischer
Design and production: Nancy Taylor
Typesetting: Alphagraphics

Zephyr Press
P.O. Box 66006
Tucson, Arizona 85728-6006

Library of Congress Cataloging-in-Publication Data
Myers, Robert E., 1924-
    Facing the Issues : creative strategies for probing critical social concerns /
  Robert E. Myers.
      p.   cm.
    Includes bibliographical references.
    ISBN 1-56976-009-8 (alk. paper)
    1. Social sciences—Problems, exercises, etc. 2. Social problems-
-Study and teaching—Activity programs. I. Title.
H62.3.M9   1995
361.1—dc20   94-28032

Contents

Contents

Contents

Contents

Foreword

This book presents in a conventional—that is, sequential—form many of the fundamental issues of the social studies curriculum. Although the lessons are logically arranged and will be easily grasped by your students, each encourages them to think in ways not always called for in "doing" social studies. We usually label the various thinking processes invoked in these materials as "creative." The processes include such diverse skills as thinking flexibly, originally, and fluently; elaborating; producing humor; abstracting; combining and synthesizing; and putting ideas into context.

The ideas and issues your students will encounter in the book are among the most important that young people can consider: freedom of speech, technological change, poverty, global warming, endangered species, our mobile society, taking responsibility for one's actions, withholding judgment, and genetic engineering. There has been no attempt to feature the "top 50" concepts and issues of the social studies curriculum, but the topics were chosen in the belief that they are timely and timeless.

We have found that when young people are given the green light and encouraged to express themselves creatively, their creative thinking abilities improve rapidly. Apparently the key factor is the teacher's attitude toward self-expression. Generally speaking, young people want to please, or comply with, their teachers, so they respond naturally and directly to the teachers' priorities. If the teachers value imaginative thinking, there is every likelihood their students will respond by being more imaginative than they would be for teachers who value conformity.

The fifty-two units that comprise *Facing the Issues* were devised with the goal of "freeing up" the creative abilities of students while helping them look at a number of important social issues. These issues are being widely discussed now, and they will continue to be discussed for many years to come. We believe that by allowing your students to tinker with concepts, to probe, to experiment, to role-play, to investigate, and to play games they will learn more about the issues than by merely reading about them.

To the Teacher

The Plan for the Units

The units in this book follow a pattern. It is a pattern that is based upon the creative thinking process. Each unit usually has three parts or levels. The first part is designed to "warm up" the student, that is, get him or her to think about a social studies topic or to engage in a certain kind of thinking. This initiating stage is all important because creative thinking can occur only when the individual can play around with ideas and let one thing lead naturally to another. At the second stage the student gets more involved in the topic, digging deeper. There is an invitation at the third stage for the student to do some thinking and doing. If we are successful in getting him or her interested in the topic, then investigating, writing, or sketching should be a natural outcome of the thinking that has been generated.

The First Level

The warm-up is a well-established and necessary part of the creative thinking process, and we believe it is especially important in allowing young people to orient their thinking and free themselves of inhibitions. This "playing around" stage is critical for anyone who would attempt to engage in a creative endeavor. Many teachers have found that giving students the initiating or first-level activity orally is a good way to warm them up for a creative thinking experience.

In this set of units we have attempted to set the stage by contriving situations in which young people will be challenged to combine ideas and elements, redefine objects and processes, elaborate upon ideas, predict consequences, explore possibilities, and analyze ideas. In several of the units we try to concoct situations in which the student can find some humor. Along with a playful attitude, a sense of humor is a wonderful lubricant for freeing a flow of original ideas.

To the Teacher

The Second Level

At the second stage the student generally is taken a little deeper into the subject that has been presented in the initiating activity. At this level we push slightly to get the student more involved in thinking about whatever he or she has been dealing with. If our questions, challenges, or requests fail, it is less likely that there will be much genuine thinking and doing by the student when he or she reaches the third level.

The Third Level

It is quite possible that a class or an individual student won't readily accept our invitation to produce something at the third level. You may regard a refusal to go ahead and come up with an idea as a failure on our part or on the student's part. It's difficult not to feel that way when students don't "go for the bait." On the other hand, there is an overwhelming amount of evidence that suggests that in creative thinking activities it is probably wise not to demand a product. The results are too often unsatisfactory for everyone concerned when we insist that a young person produce a certain kind of response. We advise you to encourage but not to insist.

The units in *Facing the Issues* will appeal to some of your students more than to others, just as some curricular activities fascinate some young people but bore others. You should, however, discover that students who generally aren't enthusiastic about regular assignments come alive when they are freed by a creative thinking activity. One of your rewards for engaging your students in activities such as these is to see someone who has been indifferent suddenly begin to shine brightly.

Since to engage in creative thinking is to rely primarily upon one's own resources, it follows that the individual student must have *practice* in expressing herself or himself in order to become an independent thinker. The principal function of this book is to provide a number of opportunities for students of widely varying talents and backgrounds to have regular experiences in thinking for themselves about social issues.

1

Needs and Wants

Noting the Contrast between Affluent and Poor Societies

Overview of the Unit

This unit has a rather obvious message. It might be hard for you to predict whether each of your students will get the message. It is impossible for us to predict, of course, since we don't know your students. The message is as follows: In a so-called affluent society, people of all ages often confuse wants and needs. Advertising plays an important role in blurring the distinction. It is easier to identify needs in countries where getting enough to eat every day is the principal concern of a majority of the people.

After a discussion of needs and wants, we present your students with a typical classroom task—classifying items. In this instance, they are to select items that we have listed and put them into columns headed by "Needs" and "Wants." Then they are asked how young people of their age might sort the same items in the future.

Idea: A Marked Contrast between Affluent and Poor Societies Exists

There are perhaps no social studies in the secondary and post-secondary curricula that don't include this theme. Regardless of whether the subject to be examined is the current sociological scene of the United States, Great Britain, Canada, Mexico, Germany, or Japan, the contrast between the haves and have-nots is ever-present. We place the focus of the problem upon the individual student and hope that the student can extrapolate to other situations, large and small.

Creative Thinking Skill to Be Developed: Orienting to the Future

One of Torrance's (Torrance and Safter 1990) eighteen creative thinking skills is "orienting to the future." He sees projecting oneself and society into future situations as being a skill that can be developed through such activities as his Future Problem Solving competitions. To be able to cope with rapid technological and sociological changes, our leaders are going to have to call upon their creative problem-solving skills and ingenuity. We can give young people practice in making extrapolations from today's trends and then trying to forecast what will happen when they meet the challenges of the future.

Preparing for the Unit

Every teacher has his or her own style, so we are really quite presumptuous in making suggestions as to how these units might be presented. With the hope that our suggestions will be taken as only ideas tossed out to stimulate your own thinking, we'll offer an idea or two about how each unit can be introduced and administered to your students. Many teachers habitually ignore teacher guides, we know, so we figure that those teachers who are curious about what we had in mind with these units will be the ones who will pay attention to our suggestions.

In the case of "Needs and Wants," the fact that it is a rather traditional exercise makes us want to recommend a more offbeat approach when you introduce it. Your approach can take the form of a little quiz, for example. You can show a big ad for a Mercedes and ask, "Would this ad ever appear in a Haitian newspaper or magazine?" (The answer is yes! Even in the poorest countries, where a majority of the people are destitute, there are wealthy people.) Or perhaps your approach can take the form of a bit of dramatics. You might ask if your students have any extra pencils because you know of a village in Baja, California, where the students don't have pencils and want very much to have some. Either approach could lead into a lively discussion about what things constitute the basic necessities of life in various areas of the world, including the diverse communities in our own country.

Presenting the Unit

Sorting out needs from wants on the list provided in the unit is an individual activity, so you should probably put your students on their own after the initiating discussion has brought them to the unit itself. If you choose not to introduce "Needs and Wants" and just hand out the unit, there is enough of a warm-up at the beginning to get your students thinking about disparities in the ways people live.

The final level, in which your students are to project themselves into the future and predict how young people would react to the same task of distinguishing needs from wants, should also be left to the individual student. As is typical of the units in *Facing the Issues,* a general discussion eliciting the various viewpoints of your students (after they have all finished the unit) will probably be well worth the time devoted to it.

Reference

Torrance, E. Paul, and H. Tammy Safter. 1993. *Making the Creative Leap Beyond.* Buffalo, N.Y.: Bearly Limited

1 Needs and Wants

1 The most important distinction in the world today is the distinction between wants and needs. For part of the world's population, wants are primary considerations. The other part is constantly concerned with needs.

What are "wants"?

What are "needs"?

Maybe you haven't even been aware of the difference between wants and needs. To you, wants may seem to be needs, thanks to the pervasiveness and effectiveness of advertising. Let's see if you can tell the differences between wants and needs. Here are some materials, events, and processes that, depending upon the situation, might be considered wants or needs. Considering only your own life, put these items in the two columns headed by the words "Wants" and "Needs."

Facing the Issues © 1994 Zephyr Press, Tucson, Arizona

Needs and Wants *(continued)*

	NEEDS	WANTS
water	_____	_____
weekends off from school	_____	_____
television	_____	_____
clothing	_____	_____
air	_____	_____
shelter	_____	_____
vegetables	_____	_____
paper	_____	_____
physical exercise	_____	_____
newspapers	_____	_____
faith in a higher authority	_____	_____
automobiles	_____	_____
summer vacations	_____	_____
pets	_____	_____
music	_____	_____
weapons	_____	_____
books	_____	_____
grains	_____	_____
sunshine	_____	_____
milk	_____	_____
sleep	_____	_____
furniture	_____	_____
fruits	_____	_____
medicine	_____	_____
meat	_____	_____
contact with other human beings	_____	_____
sporting contests	_____	_____
electricity	_____	_____
airplanes	_____	_____
moving pictures	_____	_____

2 What does the expression "freedom from want" mean?

3 Would you arrange the items into the two columns in exactly the same way when you are fifty years old? _____ Why or why not?

Would people of your age a hundred years from now arrange the items differently from the way you have? _____ Which items might be changed? Tell why they might be changed.

2

Temporary Insanity

Dealing with Freedom
of Speech and Judgment

Overview of the Unit

The story of the talented young woman who was fired for writing about the bizarre behavior of temporary employees in her office is quite true. We have simply presented the essential facts to your students and asked them to consider the feelings of all who were affected by the publication of the humorous piece and the aftermath. The daily newspaper, as many have pointed out, is an amazing collection of items of what is important and trivial in the lives of its readers. As a source of ideas for novelists, essayists, dramatists, and even poets, the newspaper is without equal. If we can believe mystery writers, a good proportion of their ideas are gleaned from the daily newspaper. It was in that tradition that "Temporary Insanity" was written. The account of the fired office worker is as accurate as we could make it. What your students make of it we can only guess.

The unit begins with a summary of the events leading up to the dismissal of the office worker. Your students are then asked in turn what their reactions would be if they were the aggrieved young woman, one of the persons she wrote about, and the office manager who did the firing.

Idea: We Are Not Always Free
to Speak Completely Freely

From time to time, this issue is a very hot one in our country, especially with regard to the media (usually the press). It is reasonable to assume that a controversy about freedom of speech will be surfacing, simmering, or even raging when the story of the fired office worker/writer is presented to your students. The First Amendment is likely to be a terribly important issue for as long as the United States exists as a republic.

Creative Thinking Skills to Be Developed: Looking from a Different Perspective; Being Flexible

The creative thinking skills to be used in this unit are looking from a different perspective and being flexible. The main purpose of "Temporary Insanity" is to have your students look at something from several angles. As in the role-reversal techniques of role-playing, your students are asked to change hats and look at the dispute from opposing viewpoints. When the role-reversal technique is successful, it can be eye-opening for the participants. We hope that will be the case for your students in attempting to imagine the feelings and thinking of three of the individuals involved in the story.

Although it is possible to exaggerate the machinations, tensions, and rivalries of office life, as a microcosm of human virtues and shortcomings it is hard to beat. By asking your students to shift their points of view and take on the feelings and thinking of one of the temporary workers and of the office manager, we hope to encourage them to be more flexible in their thinking. This adaptability aspect of flexibility is also important for teachers. We make the point in *Creative Learning and Teaching* (1970) that teachers should be able to put themselves in the places of students, administrators, and other teachers when things aren't going their way.

The basic issue raised in this unit is one of freedom of speech, and the secondary issue is exercising judgment. For most young people, the first issue is of supreme importance. They have yet to realize the importance of discretion and judgment in the overall scheme of things.

Preparing for the Unit

This activity fits in with curriculum units concerning critical thinking, business ethics, conflict resolutions, and freedom of speech. (The young woman, we note in "Temporary Insanity," did not disclose the name of her place of business or the employment agency in her column. She did contact the American Civil Liberties Union after she was dismissed.) Since the unit deals with some basic problems in human relationships, it most likely can be used in a variety of contexts in the social studies curriculum.

As stated, the issue of freedom of expression is intrinsic to the conflict between the office worker and her supervisor. Accordingly, there should be many times during the year when this unit could follow a discussion of someone defending the right to express a belief publicly. You also may be studying historical personages whose judgment in crucial situations was either questionable or controversial. Similarly, for followers of fictional dramas, whether in the classic literature or in some soap operas and situation comedies on television, there are countless instances when personal judgment makes a critical difference in the course of events.

Presenting the Unit

Most people will tend to be sympathetic to the fired worker, but there are other ways to regard her behavior and that of her supervisor. You might play devil's advocate in a discussion and take the side of the supervisor. As we hope to point out in the unit, there are many ways to look at the young woman's dismissal. In spite of one's attempts to keep an open mind, however, it is difficult not to take sides. Therefore, the unit should elicit a lively discussion if you choose to present it orally. All of the parts of the unit up to the last one might be conducted as a class discussion. In that last section, your students should probably be encouraged to digest the arguments that have been put forth and then come up with their own ideas about how this sort of problem can be resolved in the future.

You might want to engage your students in a role-playing session following the completion of the unit. Our guess is that the majority of your students will be on the side of the fired office worker. If there are any who can see a justification for her dismissal, you can set up a simple role-playing session with the backers of the two sides acting out a confrontation in the office manager's private office. Then, as we suggest above, it might be instructive to have the opponents exchange places. The little drama then can be re-enacted with different students taking the roles.

Following through with the Unit

These are possible activities for following through with a unit such as "Temporary Insanity":

1. Students share ideas about the topic in a general discussion.
2. You suggest further investigation of the topic, including interviewing.
3. Students who are motivated create a skit portraying a critical element in the controversy. Music can accompany the dramatic action.
4. Various kinds of writing grow out of the unit (for example, riddles, limericks, short stories, and essays).
5. You suggest students depict the topic in pencil, crayon, felt pen, or other medium, or students create such a depiction spontaneously.
6. Students organize a debate that brings out the various points of both sides of the controversy.
7. Pairs discuss the key points of the topic.

Reference

Torrance, E. Paul, and Robert E. Myers. 1970. *Creative Learning and Teaching.* New York: Harper.

2 Temporary Insanity

1   A young woman wrote a very humorous piece for a local newspaper in which she related some examples of bizarre behavior exhibited by a number of temporary employees

her place of business had hired. All of the people had been hired through an agency specializing in temporary help. The column did not mention the name of the business or the name of the employment agency. Nonetheless, when several people familiar with the business pointed out to the office manager that it was obvious to them that the column was about that place of business, the office manager fired the young woman, even though the office manager had recently called her "a great asset to the business."

The results of her writing true incidents in a column meant to amuse rather than to humiliate were unexpected by the young woman. At age twenty-five, she is able to obtain another position, but will this experience make her more judicious and more aware of the feelings of her supervisor, or cynical about how thin-skinned people can be?

If you were the young woman, would you be repentant, philosophical, outraged, chagrined, or a combination of these emotional states? Explain your feelings.

If you were one of the temporary employees who were portrayed in the column (the young woman's description showed their "quirkiness"), how would you regard her firing?

If you were the office manager, what would be your attitude concerning the many critical telephone calls you received after the newspaper carried the story of the young woman's firing?

2 There are several ways to look at this true story, then. Is there yet *another* perspective you can take? What is it? Explain why you would take it.

3 Having given this controversy considerable thought, what procedures do you foresee in resolving problems such as this one in the future?

3

To Success

Dealing with Relative Values

Overview of the Unit

A society can be defined by how it measures success. Is an individual successful because of accumulated wealth? Fame? Good works? Many children? A virtuous character? "To Success" raises these questions. An introduction leads into brief descriptions of ten people. Each could be considered successful by certain criteria, but it is the student's task to determine the success of the people in the descriptions relative to one another.

Idea: Values, to a Great Extent, Shape Behavior

The topic of the unit is success and how it can be measured. This idea brings forth the notion of values and valuing. Since valuing is explicit or implicit in everything we do and say, the concept elicited here can be applied to any situation that is likely to be discussed in your classroom. Is it important to study hard in order to gain access to higher education and a good job? Which is more important—looking good, that is, appearing in the most fashionable clothes and hair style, or saving for something that is fervently desired? The examples you cite in a summing-up session for this unit will come readily to your mind.

Creative Thinking Skill to Be Developed:
Looking from a Different Perspective

The first part of "To Success" calls for the critical thinking skill of making judgments. In the second part, your students are encouraged to think creatively and to see things from a different perspective. Critical and creative thinking are only antithetical when judging is premature. Evaluating has a valuable role to play in creative production, but it should come in the later stages of the creative process. When evaluation is premature, it can nip true creativity in the bud.

Preparing for and Presenting the Unit

This unit is the type that can be utilized effectively when students are studying contemporary society's values, ethics, economics, or sociology. There should be any number of class discussions—from those about celebrities to those about the power of the media—that can serve as warmups for "To Success."

Since this unit requires more reading than most of the units in *Facing the Issues,* you may elect to have your students complete the entire unit without interruption. A general discussion can follow when all of them have had enough time to reflect upon the ten individuals and debate silently to themselves as to which are truly successful.

Following through with the Unit

Depending upon the age of your students and their willingness to engage in activities such as role-playing and sketching, you might suggest that they give their impressions of any one, or a combination, of the ten individuals in a skit, a series of drawings (perhaps a mural), or limericks. A simple follow-up would be for you to suggest that they just give names to the individuals. Actually, naming them may lead naturally to the writing of limericks. We offer these suggestions only in the event that the unit is received by your students with more than average interest.

3 To Success: Looking at It Another Way

1 What many of us are looking for in life is success. But success to some is winning first prize (second prize is not winning!), and to others success is overcoming inadequacies and defects within themselves. The definition of success, then, can be quite different for various individuals. When expectations for victory are high, as they are in the Olympic Games, athletes have been known to become severely depressed because their fans reacted to their second- and third-place finishes as if they were failures. In contrast, many people feel that just to be able to finish a marathon is a glorious victory for them.

What is success to you? Is it winning, participating, or overcoming obstacles? Or is it being alive and being able to cope with life's vicissitudes?

2 Here are ten people who may or may not be considered successes. Tell whether you think each person is or is not a successful individual. Then explain why you think so.

Facing the Issues © 1994 Zephyr Press, Tucson, Arizona

1. He was the 1,003rd person to reach the summit of a 14,000-foot mountain. The other 1,002 were not handicapped. He is forty-three and has an artificial leg. For the past nine years he has been a book-keeper, and his salary is modest. His wife of eight years is a secretary; they have a daughter, three years of age.

2. He was the 248th person to reach the summit of the same mountain. It was his 24th summit at the time, and since then he has climbed 13 more. He is now thirty-seven and is considered one of the best mountain climbers in the region. As a landscape architect, his income is above average, but he didn't finish high school.

3. He was the 1,008th person to reach the summit of that mountain. He has been climbing for only five years. A grandfather and retired pharmacist, he is seventy-eight years old.

4. He is a multimillionaire and forty years old. He has gone bankrupt twice, coming away on each occasion with not much more than the clothes on his back. Each time his wits and determination have enabled him to come back and build another fortune. He was recently married for the fourth time.

5. He is a millionaire and leads a hectic life. At fifty-one, he is a prominent member of his city's most exclusive club, and his name often appears in the newspaper. Last year his wife divorced him for his failing to be a husband to her and a father to their two sons. He has been hurt by the divorce, but he is still able to do exceedingly well with his business interests.

6. He is a person with only a minimum number of possessions. He and his wife of twenty-five years rent a house now, whereas once he owned two mansions. He has no children. When his business went under, he told his creditors that he would pay back all of his debts at 100 cents on the dollar. In three years he may be able to finally pay off the last debt, having devoted almost half of his salary to debt payments for many years.

7. She is a talented poet. About a dozen of her poems have been published in small publications that print poems and other short pieces. At the age of thirty-four, she has never been paid for the publication of any of her poetry. Her husband is a very successful lawyer. She and her husband are the proud owners of three dogs and four cats; they have no children.

8. She is one of only three women admitted to a professional society of chemists in her country, a small republic in Central America. At twenty-nine, she has been credited with two minor breakthroughs in her specialty, the production of synthetic fluids. One of seven children from a poor home, she has been very busy to date and has never had a serious suitor.

9. She was Realtor of the Month five times in the past two years. Three years ago she was named Citizen of the Year, largely because of her efforts to help homeless people in her community. She has two young children, both of whom attend private schools in another state. Her husband is a maintenance worker at the local college.

10. She is just about to retire after teaching young children for forty-three years. She has never married. She is a devoted aunt to five nieces and four nephews. During her long teaching career she has never been given any particular recognition, but there will be a banquet in her honor on the Saturday after her last teaching day, and a plaque commemorating her service to the school will be put up in the hallway near the main office. The banquet and the plaque are the ideas of her former pupils.

3 Which of the ten persons described above would be considered by most people to be definitely a "success"?

Which of those ten persons would be considered a "failure" by most people?

Is it possible that none of those people considers him- or herself a success?

Which of them is most likely to believe that he or she is a failure?

Which one is likely to be firmly convinced that he or she is a success?

Many people spend a good deal of time wishing they could be someone else. There have been a great many wonderful tales told that point out the futility of that kind of wishing. Nevertheless, among those people described in this unit, two or three would probably change places with one or more of the others. Which ones would be most likely to want to change places and who would they choose as the ones whose shoes they would step into? Why?

4

100 MPG Cars

Envisioning Technological Changes

Overview of the Unit

This unit is comprised of a discussion of an ultralight car that might be produced in the future. The discussion is followed by ten questions about what the consequences would be if the car became popular.

The article upon which this activity is based appeared in newspapers throughout the country on February 17, 1993. Some of the questions asked in the unit were also posed in the article; for example, if auto makers were willing to make these ultralight cars and they caught on with the public, would there be a decline in the living standards of the workers who produce them? An expert said that making the plastic mold for the cars requires "less labor and less skilled labor at that."

Idea: An Ultralight Car Will Revolutionize Travel and Have Far-reaching Consequences

At the close of World War II there was a good deal of discussion about how helicopters would soon revolutionize travel. Heliports would be on top of every urban building. For better or worse, it didn't happen. But it fired a lot of imaginations. Perhaps ultralight cars really will change society. The idea should prove very interesting to your students.

Creative Thinking Skill to Be Developed: Anticipating Consequences

Surveys, analyses of relevant data, computerized projections, historical reviews, and hunches are all used in anticipating the consequences of introducing a new element into a specified environment. When computers are used, it is often assumed that what is projected will most likely come true; but the computer, no matter how powerful, just uses the data that it is fed. Your students might do just as well in anticipating the consequences of the successful introduction of an ultralight car, because they may see consequences resulting from the human factors that can't be quantified very well, if at all.

Preparing for the Unit

Depending upon the makeup of your class, this activity could reach students who otherwise are indifferent to playing with words in one way or another. It might mean more to a youngster who has a parent working at a job that is subject to the kind of layoff that results from technological change. It could also have some meaning for a young person who is contemplating a career in manufacturing.

If an unfortunate layoff of workers occurs either locally or nationally, you will have an excellent opportunity to administer this unit to your class. Even if your students aren't directly affected by layoffs, they should understand that evolving technology does have an impact on their lives. And, of course, cars are always a popular topic with young people.

Presenting the Unit

We offer ten categories of people whose lives could be changed greatly or minimally by the widespread acceptance of an ultralight automobile. If your students seriously consider the consequences for each group, it will take a considerable amount of thinking and writing for them to respond adequately. Accordingly, we suggest that you have them tackle the first five groups in one class session and the rest in the next class session. Having them write during the first session and then discuss the consequences for the five diverse groups is probably preferable to having your students only discuss their ideas as you lead them orally through the activity, because the more vocal students may dominate the discussion, preventing others from developing their ideas.

Following through with the Unit

For creative thinking to occur and to continue to occur, there must be ample opportunity for one thing to lead to another and for your students to do something with the information. Therefore, it is inevitable that any genuine encouragement of creative thinking in schools must take students beyond the classroom, textbook, and the teacher. An idea sparked by this unit can stimulate students to delve into the many implications of the ultralight car's impact upon our society. This delving may take the form of interviewing people, looking into various publications, or making mathematical projections on a calculator or computer. There are any number of activities that can naturally follow a unit of this kind.

4 100 MPG Cars

Anticipating Consequences

General Motors unveiled an ultralight car in January of 1992 that got 100 miles per gallon at a speed of 50 miles per hour. The car could accelerate as quickly as a sports car and could drive coast-to-coast on 29 gallons of gasoline. This ultralight car comfortably accommodates four large adults, has only one one-hundredth as many body parts as a conventional car, and, because it doesn't rust, can last for decades.

If the ultralight car becomes the most popular vehicle in the country, what would the effects be on the following:

auto body repair shop owners

manufacturers of electric cars

assembly-line workers in the auto industry

stockholders of corporations in the petroleum industry

100 MPG Cars *(continued)*

beach bums in California and Hawaii

commuters in New Hampshire in the winter

commuters in the metropolitan Seattle area

rock musicians

firefighters

people earning the minimum wage

5

When the Floods Come

Contemplating a Relief Measure as a Result of Global Warming

Overview of the Unit

This unit is gloomy in its basic prediction of cataclysmic floods but optimistic about the kind of cooperation the world's peoples might engage in if a catastrophe of the kind described in the unit were ever to happen. Your students are to consider what kind of televised musical event would be best to raise money for the relief of the multitudes of people who would be displaced by the floods.

Idea: Worldwide Cooperation May Be Crucial if There Is a Global Disaster

There are several themes inherent in this unit—global warming, entertainment, and technology among them—but the underlying idea put forth is that of worldwide cooperation. Some experts claim that if the peoples of the Earth are to be saved from disasters accompanying global warming there will have to be a very real cooperation among the nations of the world.

Creative Thinking Skills to Be Developed: Combining Ideas and Elements; Being Original

The basic task confronting your students in completing this unit is to combine the music of a diverse group of musicians into a program with "universal" appeal. No easy task. The combining skill in this case is more like arranging costumes sequentially in a fashion show and not so much like mixing the ingredients of a tasty dish.

The original element in the unit is found in the thinking that must go into making the selections to be presented. The kinds of musical extravaganzas held in the past won't be suitable for this occasion. There must be an ingenious mixture of music, the rhythms, melodies, and harmonies of which appeal to the basic musical needs of all people.

Preparing for the Unit

Having a discussion of global warming and the "greenhouse effect" would be a wonderful way to introduce this unit. Since that problem isn't likely to be solved very quickly, it may crop up at any time you and your students are discussing world affairs.

If you are inclined to do so, you might investigate the status of the global warming problem before introducing the subject. Scientists are still divided as to the seriousness of the problem—at least at this writing they are.

Presenting the Unit

In all probability a discussion leading into the unit is all that you need, aside from giving your students the signal to go ahead with the activity. This kind of activity, however, cries for a class discussion once it is completed. Your students will advance many differing musical menus, and comparing them should be entertaining and informative. You will have a number of clues as to how to handle the discussion as it proceeds. There may be some heated arguments, so the level of the discussion must be kept on an impersonal plane.

5 When the Floods Come

Let's say you are to be the organizer of a "music spectacular" that will be televised worldwide as a benefit for people dislocated by the rising seas that have flooded land all over the globe. The "greenhouse effect" has raised the level of the waters that comprise most of the Earth's surface, and there have been countless deaths and dislocations of families. Funds for food, clothing, and housing are desperately needed, so a number of fund-raising events are planned. Your two-hour program will be one of the key events in the series of events designed to bring in unprecedented amounts of money.

Since the telecast is to be seen worldwide, you believe the program must be universal in its appeal and feature excellent examples of all kinds of music. Thanks to the consortium of television networks formed for this purpose, you have a generous budget for transporting the musicians from wherever they live to the filming location.

What will be the kinds of music you will have on your program? You expect every musician to volunteer his or her services and to receive a fair reimbursement for expenses, but each musician will also have ideas about what will go over big with a worldwide audience. You may have some huge egos to contend with. When you and your staff finally put the program together, what will it look like?

When the Floods Come (continued)

Do a little research and then make some decisions about which kinds of music will have a very wide appeal. There must be considerable variety in the musical offerings, but you must not risk losing a large portion of your audience by programming selections back-to-back that don't appeal to a majority of the viewers. Take into account that tastes in music, as in everything else, change and may be different "when the floods come." Create a program that you think will be successful.

Facing the Issues © 1994 Zephyr Press, Tucson, Arizona

6
Martin

Reflecting on Illiteracy among the Aged

Overview of the Unit

"Martin" is comprised of a story of a seemingly well-adjusted man who is illiterate and some questions about how the problem of illiteracy might be dealt with fifty years from now. The student is asked if presently any educational programs exist in other countries that have a higher success rate in producing literate citizens than the U.S. program. At this writing, Japan's program is far more successful.

Idea: Illiteracy among the Aged Is Part of a Bigger Problem

Illiteracy is a controversial matter these days. Are there really as many people, young and old, who are functional illiterates in this country as is being claimed? If students look at the problem, they can have several reactions. Being immersed in a milieu that is still very much oriented to written language, students may marvel that people can get by without being able to read and write. On the other hand, some students are very deficient in those skills themselves, faking it throughout their school years.

It is both tragic and amusing to consider what happens when a student who is unable to read and to write is confronted with a lesson such as this one. If such a student "opens up" about the problems of pretending to handle curricular material requiring the ability to respond in other than an oral fashion, a great deal of light can be shed upon one important problem of the modern secondary school. From the evidence we have of people such as Martin and other nonreading adults being taught to read, there is considerable hope that the faking high school students in this country can become genuinely literate.

Creative Thinking Skill to Be Developed: Being Sensitive and Aware

Our purpose in this unit is to make the student more aware of a real problem in our country, that of illiteracy. So many adults (and children) fake the ability to comprehend written language that your students may not realize the seriousness of the problem. Programs for helping adults learn how to read have burgeoned in the past two decades, but the problem isn't licked by any means. The skill of being sensitive and aware is really only one part of a process that is accompanied by *wanting to do something* as a result of the newly felt awareness. If even one of your students has a genuine desire to help someone learn how to read, this unit will have been enormously successful.

Preparing for the Unit

This is one of a few units in the book that have a lengthy introduction. The introduction is a short story about an illiterate man. Although you may have a serendipitous opportunity to lead into this unit when a topic of literacy, drop-outs, or international business competition comes up, the story at the beginning of the unit can serve as the warm-up, with just a word or two of introduction from you. It might be a good idea to ask your students if they know anyone like the man in the story they are about to read. When they have completed the unit, it should prove interesting if any of them knows someone like Martin.

Presenting the Unit

Unless you decide to read the story aloud, your students can be put on their own when this unit is first presented. You should have some general discussion about the illiteracy problem, however. In spite of many recent newspaper and magazine articles about illiteracy, we'll bet that some of your students are unaware of the prevalence of illiteracy in this country. If one of your students does know someone similar to Martin, this unit can "come alive" as an educational experience.

6 Martin

Martin was eighty-five years old, but he didn't act like it. He would get on a ladder to fix the roof of his house. He'd also walk two miles to town to deposit his monthly check at the utilities office. When the weather was fair, he would ride his bicycle across town to see his friend, Jessica, age sixty-nine. In the summer, if he felt particularly frisky, he would take a swim in the lake a block from his house. Martin amazed his friends and neighbors.

Martin had only one obvious failing: he was illiterate. Since he lived alone, the fact that he couldn't read posed many problems. He couldn't read his bills very well, although he knew what the numbers meant. He didn't know what to make of the notice from the election board about where he was to vote now that his precinct had been changed. Once he found out where to go, he had to be assisted in making up his mind about the various candidates running for office and the propositions being put forth for the voters' approval. Even though he had a cheerful disposition, Martin was becoming more irritable since his wife had died. She had helped him when something needed to be read. Now, it seemed, there were too many problems concerning reading, and Martin was convinced that he was too old to learn how.

Illiteracy *is* a huge problem for more people than our society cares to admit. But since there is more and more emphasis placed upon using personal computers and other electronic communications devices, perhaps there won't be very many "Martins" fifty years from now. In going through any educational program, the individual student could be assured of learning to read and to write.

Of course, children who don't go to school or receive home instruction can still grow up and be illiterate. Is there any country in the world now where illiteracy is almost unknown? If so, how does that country manage to get nearly everyone to learn to read and to write?

How will illiteracy be handled in the future? What will be the factors that will affect basic education in the first part of the twenty-first century? Do some research in order to make "informed guesses" about education's future.

Facing the Issues © 1994 Zephyr Press, Tucson, Arizona

7

Cravings

Taking Another Look at Addictions

Overview of the Unit

"Cravings" is just a simple exercise in producing ideas. The subject is the strong desires that people possibly will develop for electronic entertainment in the future. Intrinsic in this kind of craving are the needs for amusement, companionship, diversion, and escape, among others. Television, for example, has proved to be addictive. Your students are invited to think of ways that people will be hooked by electronic devices in the future.

Idea: Some Addictions of the Future May Be in the Area of Entertainment

Undoubtedly, many physiological and psychological cravings exist today that were unknown in other times. It is likely that new cravings—some of which will be quite powerful—will greatly affect the behavior of people in the future. The possibility of people craving certain kinds of entertainment may not seem far-fetched to your students, who may well be "hooked" on certain electronic devices now.

Creative Thinking Skill to Be Developed: Being Fluent

A flow of good ideas is essential to thinking creatively. If the first idea to occur doesn't work, other ideas must be forthcoming. Ideational fluency can be developed by means of a series of experiences in which the individual learns to let go, to associate ideas freely, and to remove inhibiting sets. Although this unit in itself is not sufficient to make an appreciable difference in the ability of the individual to think fluently, it is an example of an activity that has long been used for that purpose.

Preparing for the Unit

The tie-in for this unit can be any discussion of the subjects of addiction, television, electronic games, or entertainment. "Cravings" probably does need an introduction of some kind, even though it deals with two very common topics, namely, entertainment and cravings (addictions). It probably won't be necessary to explore addictions very thoroughly in connection with this unit because that subject is discussed so often. You should make the point, however, that some psychological addictions are almost as powerful as physical addictions.

Presenting the Unit

Since it is unlikely that the actual listing done by the student at the end of the unit will take a great deal of time, your introduction, administration, and follow-up discussion can be fitted nicely into a class period. A discussion following completion of the unit is advisable because it can be the vehicle for sorting out ideas about the psychological needs that all young people in this country are developing in an age dominated increasingly by electronic media.

Encouraging Independent Thinking and Doing

In order to provide the kind of setting in which young people can grow intellectually, during and after the administration of these units you can encourage your students to

- become more aware of problems and difficulties
- accept limitations constructively, as a challenge, improvising with what is available, rather than cynically
- build upon their talents and strengths
- deliberately and systematically elaborate upon the information they receive
- perceive information as incomplete; try to fill in the gaps

- juxtapose apparently irrelevant elements
- explore mysteries
- make predictions from limited information
- search for truth and wisdom
- visualize relationships, processes, and anticipated events
- use more than one sense modality in being sensitive to and solving problems
- appreciate and use humor

7 Cravings

Pregnant women are known for having cravings for pickles, chocolate, sauerkraut, and other foods. Cravings are intense desires that sometimes drive people to behave in peculiar ways. When one has a craving, one has the compulsion to attain a goal, and attaining the goal once is usually not enough to satisfy the craving. There are cravings for a wide variety of things other than food. We can crave music, love, sympathy, excitement, attention, solitude, and much more.

Throughout history, humanity's physiological and psychological needs have determined most of the cravings people have experienced. With the coming of the electronic age, it is possible that some new cravings are appearing. Young people especially may develop cravings in the field of entertainment that were unknown a generation or two ago. These cravings may be as genuine as the compulsions some people feel for chocolate or attention.

Think of as many kinds of cravings as you can that could crop up in the future in the field of entertainment and list them below.

Facing the Issues © 1994 Zephyr Press, Tucson, Arizona

8

Kill the Messenger

Dealing with Responsibility

Overview of the Unit

This unit is closely related to "Blame" (17). The natural tendency in humans is to look for someone or something other than ourselves to blame. Accepting full responsibility for our actions is difficult for most of us. The problem dealt with in "Kill the Messenger" is the ways in which responsibility is accepted. In the unit we note that there are times when "the messenger," the one bringing the bad news, might justifiably be blamed.

Idea: Sometimes "Killing the Messenger" Is Justified

This unit deals with personal relationships and the concept that individuals should be responsible for their acts. There are issues involved, too. When is it all right for government officials to leak information to the press? Should newspapers report police arrests if they are not in the habit of also reporting exonerations? In the seventies colleges and universities stopped sending reports of their students' grades to parents. If the students chose not to disclose they were failing their courses, it was just a matter of their consciences and their relationships with their parents. The institutions couldn't be killed (criticized) for sending a depressing message!

Creative Thinking Skill to Be Developed:
Looking from a Different Perspective

A case can be made that "looking from a different perspective" is fundamental to the production of any new idea. Logically, if something is seen from a traditional or ordinary perspective, ideas that result are not likely to be novel. A creative person is able to view a commonplace object or situation in unique and exciting ways.

In this unit we hope to provoke your students into seeing society in a way that is different from their typical perspective. For example, when looking at the print and electronic media as responsible institutions, your students should inquire about these media's role in protecting the national interests in time of war. What about their violation of the privacy of individuals? Do the media have any responsibility for downplaying sensational crimes that are likely to be "copycatted"? Sometimes teachers will take an unpopular position on an issue in order to strengthen their students' grasp of the factors involved, but the approach taken here is the more unusual one of combining a notion, "kill the messenger," with matters such as health information (does the Privacy Act cover all health situations?), romantic involvements, and religious experiences. To cite perhaps the most controversial of these questions, the disclosure of a teen's pregnancy to her parents has been a very hot issue among the right-to-life faction, as well as to the family-planning faction, for a number of years.

Preparing for and Presenting the Unit

We can imagine a week or more of discussions resulting from the administration of this unit. Nevertheless, at the simplest level, you can present it without much comment and with very little attention to your students' reactions. With some students, the principal reactions may be confusion and frustration. Therefore, we think one of the most important things you can do, in addition to linking the unit with the current events in the lives of your students, is to make sure the concept of killing the messenger is understood by all of your students. The notion isn't hard to grasp when you cite the ancient Greeks in this regard, but its application to today's social issues may be a little elusive for some of your students. Accordingly, a discussion is called for before your students tackle the final section of the unit.

8 Kill the Messenger

There is an old saying about people taking anger out on the messenger who brings the bad news: "They killed the messenger." Unfortunately, messengers with news of a defeat or a calamity have actually been put to death. Nothing could be more unreasonable, of course, because the messenger might have had nothing to do with creating the event that the receiver of the message so deplored.

Many, if not most, of us actually do "kill the messenger," figuratively speaking. We berate (usually to ourselves) the mail carrier who only delivers ads to our mailbox. When we pay a sales tax, we are only half-kidding when we make a cutting remark about the governor. Most of us are only joking when we condemn the television "meteorologist" for predicting rotten weather, but we do tend to identify such natural forces and events with people such as weather forecasters.

There are some occasions, on the other hand, when the bearer of sad tidings or gossip might legitimately be blamed. Have you ever realized that the person who told you that so-and-so made a disparaging remark about you is perhaps more to be blamed than the individual who supposedly made the remark? It's generally not necessary to tell a person that someone else made a negative comment. What was the "friend's" motivation in telling you? So there <u>are</u> times when the messenger isn't so innocent.

Can you think of other times when you'd like to "kill the messenger"? What are they?

When is it justifiable to "kill the messenger"

in national emergencies?

disclosure of arrests and fines in the newspaper?

very personal information?

grades?

romantic involvements?

health information?

religious experiences?

athletic competitions?

public policy making?

financial affairs?

9
Is Bigger Better?

Taking a Close Look at Size and Growth

Overview of the Unit

There are reports from time to time that individuals who have graduated from small high schools have generally better self-concepts and tend to be better adjusted socially than individuals who graduate from large high schools. Although the claim is made by people who want to consolidate school districts and eliminate small schools that students attending those schools are underprivileged, it would appear that those students are also blessed in some important respects.

As a society we have been obsessed with bigness, but there are signs that our thinking is undergoing some modification. In this unit, we hope to have your students look critically at the notion of large size as being a goal for nearly everything. Following the introductory remarks about big versus small, we ask your students to decide whether ten items are better if they are big or small. Then, by asking them how in the future they would manage three situations affected by size, we hope to force your students to take a closer look at the idea of size.

Idea: Bigger May Not Be Better

Size is noticeable in nearly everything—in people, cities, pets, fires, trees, ad infinitum. It is important to young people whether they are large or small in stature and whether they are slim or rotund. In certain sports, such as football and basketball, size often is crucial to the individual's being allowed to play.

The tendency in most people, especially the young, is to equate bigness with superiority. With children, there are obvious advantages to largeness and disadvantages to smallness, and thus they are predisposed to seeing bigness as preferable in most matters. In the cases of gems, libraries, and generosities there is little doubt that "the bigger the better," but even in those cases largeness can have its drawbacks. The huge diamond must be guarded continuously, for example, which can be a serious drawback at times.

Creative Thinking Skill to Be Developed: Orienting to the Future

Torrance and Safter (1993) make this point: "Everyone must be a futurist. The creative mind must certainly continue to shape itself in terms of the future." In this unit we ask your students to imagine themselves in future situations that require decisions about the size of a group of people protecting whales and the size of "bubble farms." Our intention is to encourage them to look forward and imagine what life will be like when they are in their thirties and forties.

Preparing for the Unit

You may be living in a community that has been struggling with problems of growth. More and more cities are restricting the growth of residential and industrial developments because of concerns about "urban blight" and transportation problems. If your students are not living in such a community, they should at least be aware of the fact that throughout the country land use and encroachment into agricultural lands are hot issues. A brief discussion about the general problem would be ideal for leading into "Is Bigger Better?"

It is estimated that earth's human population increases by nearly 245,000 daily. By the year 2050, our planet's 5.5 billion people will have nearly doubled.

Presenting the Unit and Following Through

Depending on how well versed your students are about topics such as urban blight, bubble farms, and the plight of whales, this unit could provoke a good deal of discussion and some follow-up study. Actually, the only true measure of how successful these units are is the amount of learning that takes place *following* their administration. We believe that your encouragement is the key factor in making legitimate further investigation of topics raised in this book. Inasmuch as all of the units deal either with a vital concept or an important issue, they should be considered primarily as springboards for further learning.

Reference

Torrance, E. Paul, and Tammy Safter. 1993. *Making the Creative Leap Beyond*. Buffalo, N.Y.: Bearly Limited.

9 Is Bigger Better?

1 People in Texas, Alaska, and New York have something in common. They have been known to brag that their states are bigger, wealthier, and more beautiful than other states are. Whether they are right or not, some people resent the people in those states saying so. Maybe in self-defense, many individuals point out that smaller is sometimes much better than bigger. For example, they say that small towns don't have the traffic problems that big cities do. What are the other advantages of the small town?

2 Tell which is better, big or small, and why, for these items:

a piece of pizza

a sports car

a professional wrestler

Is Bigger Better? *(continued)*

a piece of bubble gum

a pet dog

a pet hamster

a pet cat

an audience viewing a television program

someone playing hide and seek

a lecture from an adult

a fire

a letter you write to a friend

a letter a friend writes to you

a wrapped birthday present

3 If you were a passenger in a spacecraft going to another planet, would it be better to be big or to be small? Why?

If you were in charge of a program for protecting right whales in the Atlantic Ocean to keep them from becoming extinct, would it be better to have a small staff or a big staff of helpers? Why?

If you were the planner for a "bubble farm" thirty years from now, would you want a large amount of space for one very large farm or many small areas for a series of bubble farms? Why?

Facing the Issues © 1994 Zephyr Press, Tucson, Arizona

10

The Harassed Crowd

Examining the Phenomenon of Migration

Overview of Activity

This activity is a guessing game. It is simply comprised of three questions posed to the student concerning a brief passage about a migration. After asking the initial questions concerning the identity of the migrants, we offer two simple facts, namely, the migration described took place more than a hundred years ago and it has been reported a great many times since. Finally, we ask the student whether her or his thinking about the migration would change if the description were of a "harassed" crowd 100 years hence.

Idea: Migrations Always Are Indicative of Some Kind of Change

A migration entails a moving from one place to another. As the term is usually employed, migrations involve many individuals, whether human or animal. Although almost all migrations are the result of changing conditions of weather, food, and population density, or of human oppression, the occasions when multitudes of individuals move together to some distant place never cease to fascinate us. Butterflies, eels, caribou, and ancient Asians crossing the Bering Sea are all of exceptional interest to us. So, whereas migrations are common features of life on this planet, the idea is one that stirs the imagination.

Creative Thinking Skill to Be Developed: Being Flexible

By throwing two sets of additional facts at students, we hope to force their thinking about the "harassed crowd" to accommodate the new information. We haven't changed the rules of the game, but we have caused students to adjust their thinking, adapting the original responses to the added information. By doing so, we have tried to influence students to think flexibly.

Of course, the knowledgeable student might well say "lemming" to the first question and stick to his or her guns upon encountering the second and third sets of questions. In that event, the ultimate question is: Will there still be mass migrations of lemmings one hundred years from now, or will ecological changes alter the periodic population explosions of those rodents so that migrations won't happen as they have been happening for centuries?

We are hoping, of course, that the student will conceive the actors in the drama to be human. In that case, the third set of questions provides a good deal of food for thought.

Preparing for the Unit

Timing, as the saying goes, is everything. Conceivably, "The Harassed Crowd" can be an awful disaster or a smashing success. As you know, there are no guarantees in teaching. The important thing about administering this unit is that the attitude of the class should be one of suspended judgment. That is a requirement if activities such as this one are to have any positive results. Accordingly, your role in presenting the activity is simply to enhance or to try to foster an atmosphere of scientific inquiry (on a somewhat rudimentary level). A few remarks about not jumping to conclusions or an actual anecdote about someone being embarrassed about jumping to conclusions should set the stage effectively for a satisfactory learning experience.

Presenting the Unit

Ideally, there should be some class discussion at the beginning of most of the units in this book. Depending upon how you want to use the unit, you can make the first part a general discussion or an individualized assignment. In the case of "The Harassed Crowd," there are advantages in having your students respond to the questions without a general discussion, because inevitably certain individuals influence others in a discussion, and we want the individual to do his or her own thinking. Not everyone in any given classroom is knowledgeable about lemmings, and part of the fun of the unit is imagining human beings throwing themselves into the sea.

10   The Harassed Crowd

1   "They rear their families on their journey, and the three or four generations swell into a pilgrim caravan. They winter during seven or eight weary months. At length, the harassed crowd, thinned by unending attacks, yet still a vast multitude, plunged into the sea."

What do the words above describe? What is happening?

Who are "they"?

Where is the setting?

2   Now that you have done some thinking about the actors in the drama described above, let's adjust your thinking about the migration. Those words were written more than a hundred years ago, but the migration has taken place periodically right up to our own time. Does that make you change your answers to the three questions? If so, change them now.

What do the words above describe? What is happening?

Who are "they"?

Where is the setting?

3 Can you adjust your thinking some more? Let's suppose the passage describes something that will happen *a hundred years from now.* Would you still have the same answers to those three questions? Would the drama be as likely to happen 200 years from now? Explain your reasons for either keeping your answers or changing them.

=11=
Jogging into the Future

Overview of the Unit

This unit is comprised of three problems presented to the student, as a dedicated jogger in a huge city, when circumstances change and the student's exercise program must be altered. The student must contend with changes in the neighborhoods and in city regulations in order to continue to jog.

Idea: We All Have to Breathe the Air!

Although every one of us is dependent upon the quality of the air we breathe, joggers and other athletes who compete outdoors are more aware of air quality than those of us who don't exercise vigorously outside. It is commonplace for joggers to complain about pollution and pollen, as well as about heat and cold. If animals such as the northern spotted owl are excellent indicators of the health of the forest, joggers are reliable guides in assessing the livability of our cities and towns.

Creative Thinking Skill to Be Developed: Being Flexible

In order to be able to handle changes in routine or shifting circumstances, one must be flexible. Some people are more flexible than others, of course. The truly inflexible individuals have trouble making realistic adjustments to change; they want everything and everyone to adjust to them. In contrast, creative thinkers can alter their thinking and adapt themselves, including their thinking, to new demands upon their behavior. This unit is designed to give your students a little practice in looking for alternative ways of achieving an objective.

Preparing for the Unit

You might lead into the unit with a remark or two about the frustrations people have in dealing with changes in their lives. Since everyone has frustrations, experiences by your students in coping with moving, regulations, and being disadvantaged by the mistakes of others (or even blamed for them) could possibly be among the experiences related, and all of them are in the unit.

Presenting the Unit

If you do lead in to the unit with a discussion of frustrations, you should be able to get your students ready for tackling the unit itself. The problem is that they may become too emotional to do a proper job of thinking flexibly about the three problems; they may be too interested in expressing their discontent with the "hardships" and "injustices" they have experienced. On the other hand, you want them to become the protagonist in the unit because they otherwise might view the problems as being unworthy of their serious attention.

11 Jogging into the Future

Imagine that you live in one of the world's largest cities. It is a sprawling industrial metropolis. Although poor, you are convinced of the importance of good nutrition and exercise. So you watch what you eat and jog every morning. The trouble is, the air is horribly polluted. Your solution is to wear a mask to breathe through. Unfortunately, the mask makes jogging difficult.

After two years of jogging, you find out that the neighborhood in which you live, a motley collection of small businesses, apartments, and factories, is being razed so that new high-rise office buildings can be constructed. Your usual route for jogging has been blocked off. Besides the prospect of not having a place in which to live, you have a strong urge to keep running every morning before work, but it will take you too long to bike out of the neighborhood to find another jogging route.

What can you do?

Jogging into the Future (continued)

Five years later, you have moved from the old neighborhood to one with a nearby canal that has a path for pedestrians. In spite of all the difficulties you have encountered over the years, you have maintained your exercise program. However, you are again forced to rethink your daily regimen. Because some bicyclists have knocked over pedestrians on the path you jog on, running and biking on the path are now prohibited. Your situation is worse this time because your new neighborhood is even farther away from any possible jogging route, and the sidewalks are so crowded that jogging on them is out of the question.

What can you do?

Ten years after you solved your problem in the second neighborhood, a much greater threat to your exercise program is posed. The pollution in the city's air has become so bad that everyone is forced, by law, to wear a gas mask. This mask is engineered in such a way that steady jostling movements, such as those that occur during jogging, cause the chemicals in the mask to cease functioning, and the air breathed through the mask becomes worse than if the wearer didn't have a mask on.

What can you do?

Facing the Issues © 1994 Zephyr Press, Tucson, Arizona

=12=
The Disappearing Bears

Looking at a Case of an Endangered Species of Animal

Overview of the Unit

The plight of the grizzly bear is presented to your students in this unit, and then they are asked to offer a solution to the problem. The predicament of the grizzly is real, of course, and we hope your students take it seriously.

Idea: Species of Animals and Plants Are Becoming Extinct at an Alarming Rate.

There is no need to define for your students the issue of disappearing animal and plant species. The problem receives nearly as much publicity nowadays as scandal. Nevertheless, the conservationists believe that the rate of extinction of endangered species is increasing rather than slowing down. In the context of growing concerns about a drastic reduction in the world's forests and alarming reports of increasing pollution in rivers, lakes, and oceans, this issue is one that must be reviewed by your students, who will have a say about these matters very soon.

Creative Thinking Skill to Be Developed:
Being Sensitive and Aware

Although it is quite likely that your students will have heard of the precarious situation of grizzly bears in the United States, they may not be aware of just how close we are to losing the bears because of human encroachment upon their habitat. Even though the grizzly is just one of many species that are close to extinction, your students can take a good look at the economic and ecological factors that have produced this sad situation and try to get a feeling for what is involved in issues of this kind.

Preparing for the Unit

The concerns of environment/conservation groups have been pooh-poohed by land developers, chemical manufacturers, timber companies, mining companies, and ranchers, but those concerns are being felt more and more by the public at large. There is hardly an issue of *National Wildlife, Audubon,* or *Natural History* that isn't loaded with articles about the devastation of forests, wildlife, grasslands, seas, lakes, rivers, and the air. You and your students can read the articles in those periodicals, and you can read the articles in the newspapers in connection with this unit. The issue raised in "The Disappearing Bears" is one that is being raised all over the world.

Presenting the Unit

Many have the feeling that asking young people to offer their solutions to what may seem to be insoluble problems is a futile exercise. If our elected officials and scientific organizations can't solve these problems, how can young people without power and resources help? There are two answers. The youngsters learn by digging in and finding out what the issues are all about. And by being informed, they can influence adults through direct action. Given an opportunity, young people many times have brought their thinking about significant issues to the attention of public and private officials. Land has been reclaimed, historical sites have been saved, hazards have been removed, and plants and animals have been preserved because of the actions of young people.

Guidelines for Doing Research

Following are some guidelines for doing research that your students might review before investigating the issues raised in this unit:

1. **Read**
   Read carefully. Take notes on points you think are particularly important.

2. **Think**
   Don't believe everything you read. Incorrect and misleading information is some times found in print. Examine what you read with a critical eye.

3. **Check**
   If what you read seems implausible or illogical, try to determine how valid it is by:

   comparing it with other sources of information

   deciding how reliable the material is by learning the qualifications of the author or editors

   examining the date of publication
   determining if the material is well supported

4. **Understand**
   Try to grasp the substance of the material as you read. If the author has a purpose in presenting his or her ideas, try to discover what that purpose is. Find someone, such as a teacher, parent, or librarian, who can help you interpret difficult passages. Try to get an overall idea of your material.

12 The Disappearing Bears

1 There have always been grizzly bears in Montana's Mission Mountains. But will bears still be there twenty years from now, or even ten years from now? It has been estimated that there were more than a thousand grizzlies in the areas surrounding the Mission Mountains a hundred years ago. Twenty years ago there were fewer than a hundred. Today there are ten grizzly bears left in the region.

If you extrapolate, how many bears will be in the Mission Mountains ten years from now? (Is it possible to extrapolate to zero?)

2 Here are some facts about the disappearing grizzly in Montana. If development continues in the neighboring Swan Valley, the bears will soon be gone. The Swan Valley is critical to the bears because they must pass through it to reach the Northern Continental Divide ecosystem, including the Bob Marshall Wilderness, Glacier National Park, and national parks in Canada. If the Mission Mountains are cut off from that larger ecosystem by more logging, more roads, and more vacation homes, the bears are doomed. The Mission bears are a subset of a much larger population, the Northern Continental Divide population. The Mission bears can't be separated from the population, because the Mission Mountains aren't big enough to maintain the subset on their own.

  Facing the Issues © 1994 Zephyr Press, Tucson, Arizona

The Disappearing Bears (continued)

If you want to help keep this population of grizzlies from dying out, what solution can you offer for this problem? Do some research about grizzly habitat and the ecosystem that includes the Mission grizzlies. Learn what you can about the geography of the region. Then offer at least one solution to the problem of the disappearing grizzly.

13
Painkillers

Examining Antidotes for Pain

Overview of the Unit

The topic of this unit is pain, and that is no laughing matter, as we say in the unit. We have heard of people who can laugh while a dentist pulls out their teeth—without an anesthetic—but the two elements, pain and humor, aren't usually very compatible. Nevertheless, we tried to inject some humor into what is a very serious subject, especially in citing the bad, old joke about beating your head against the wall and in mixing semi-serious, frivolous, and serious items in the last section. With so much pain in our world, we cannot hope to cope successfully with life's vicissitudes without addressing the issue of pain.

Idea: Pain Is a Significant Part of Life

Although it isn't a pleasant topic (unless one is a genuine sadist), pain is present in every aspect of life. An enormous amount of time, money, and energy is devoted to reducing or eliminating pain. Not only the enormous medical-pharmaceutical industry but healers, witch doctors, therapists, and hypnotists are enlisted by the world's human inhabitants to alleviate pain in one way or another. Your students undoubtedly know a great deal—probably too much—about physical and psychological pain. Nevertheless, we hope engaging in this unit won't be a painful experience for them.

Creative Thinking Skill to Be Developed:
Being Sensitive and Aware

Logically, individuals must be sensitive to problems and to the urgings within themselves before they can solve problems. In this unit we are asking students to play around with what must be an unpleasant topic for all but sadists and masochists. ("Playing around with ideas" is another activity necessary for people when they are creating.) The subject is ordinarily one that doesn't lend itself to a casual approach, but we have treated it rather casually to induce the student to become a little more sensitive to the social-psychological problems of our society.

Preparing for the Unit

If you can time the administering of this unit to follow a discussion of a disturbing social problem, it may bring out some insights that your students didn't know they possessed. As far as your actually introducing the unit is concerned, you shouldn't have to do much leading in, because the unit has a long introductory section. You would do well to set the stage, however, with a brief remark, perhaps along the lines that the human condition inevitably deals with pains of various kinds.

Presenting the Unit

After getting through the long introduction in the first two sections, the student is asked to come up with antidotes to various actions that some people find painful. You can make the entire unit a cooperative oral activity, or you can have students go it alone all the way. The first two parts of the unit don't really lend themselves to the usual warming-up discussion featured in most of this book's units.

One or two of the items in the last section may seem farfetched, but there really are people who are so irritated by loud gum chewing that they experience a kind of pain. (We admit that the first item about hearing a story told for the fourth time is whimsical.) The items about test taking and being lectured to were included because we wanted some emotional involvement from students who aren't motivated by their school careers. In all likelihood, having your students respond to this section independently will obviate the risk of some students getting wild or silly in a group discussion.

13 Painkillers

1 There are different kinds of pain. Nowadays when someone mentions pain it is as likely to be of the mental variety as of the physical kind. A great many people experience pain to some degree every day—those with chronic illnesses, those whose situations seem hopeless, those who are continually degraded, those whose work actually involves great physical discomfort, and others.

Just a glance at the daily newspaper will reveal that any number of people have experienced pain during the previous twenty-four hours. One of the most popular sayings among people who train in gymnasiums and run on the track or on the road is "No pain, no gain." Pain is a major component of modern living. Is a young person growing up in our society to believe that pain is a necessary or desirable ingredient in life?

2 We might look at pain as an experience that leads to another, more positive experience. Should we take seriously this old gag?

"Why are you beating your head against that wall?"

"Because it feels so good when I stop."

Painkillers *(continued)*

It is doubtful that anyone is really in pain—even though some claim to be—when he or she hears a bad pun. Nevertheless, what is the best way to respond to a bad pun?

Genuine pain, of course, is no laughing matter. It can make everything in life worse, sometimes to the degree that it is the dominant theme of a person's existence.

3 What are the countervailing experiences to pain? Pleasure? Relief from pain (as in the joke above)? What other countervailing experiences can you think of?

In the twenty-first century what might the practical antidotes for the following painful experiences be? Think of measures, materials, tactics, rejoinders, or conventions that might be more suitable for the twenty-first century than for the end of the twentieth century.

Hearing a story told for the fourth time

Hearing someone chewing gum very loudly

Being subjected to ridicule

Losing a championship game by one point

Being subjected to excruciating noise

Losing a loved one

Listening to a boring lecture

Taking an "impossible" test

Watching someone you love lie

14

A Sporting Proposal

Looking Anew at Spectator Sports

Overview of the Unit

This is a brief exercise in thinking about the essential nature of sporting events. After differentiating between games and sports, your students are invited to choose a game that might be expanded into a sport and tell how that might be accomplished.

Idea: A Game Differs from a Sport

Since spectator sports comprise such a large part of our ethos, it seems reasonable to include a unit about sports and games in this collection of important ideas and issues of our times. How much prominence to give spectator sports is the issue for many. At the very time this unit is being written, there is a report of a riot in Rotterdam. Police arrested 950 English fans "as mobs rampaged through the streets of Amsterdam and Rotterdam" after England lost a soccer match to The Netherlands.

Inasmuch as such behavior is literally not part of the sport but part of the milieu in which the sport is played, most people are not inclined to blame a spectator sport such as soccer for the unseemly behavior that the sport seems to engender. Nonetheless, why the outcomes of athletic events such as Super Bowl games and NCAA basketball championships should eventuate in riots in Chicago, San Francisco, and Detroit is something for your students to ponder.

Creative Thinking Skill to Be Developed: Elaborating

By adding to the essential features of a game and making it into a sport, your students will be elaborating upon a basic structure. In all probability, they won't be modifying the structure or nature of the game but will be adding elements so that the game can accommodate spectators and the accompanying trappings of a sport.

Preparing for the Unit

Athletic contests are always in the news, and very likely they are often the topics your students talk about in and out of class. As a society, we give a great deal of attention to sports. This unit can fit right in with an upcoming athletic event or one that has just been completed.

Presenting the Unit and Following Through

There should be a number of games your students will propose to be made more popular or accessible. Not in every instance will a favorite game be a candidate for expansion into a spectator sport, however. The virtue of some games is that they are private or quasi-private. A fair number of spectators can watch a game of horseshoes, but part of its charm is that spectators are superfluous. As a matter of fact, we aren't sure whether horseshoes can be considered a sport.

A discussion about the pervasive influence of television upon athletic contests all over the world might follow the administration of this unit. Many sports have changed in this country because of television and money (they are nearly synonymous), altering the times and the ways those sports are conducted. Because your students are young, they may take for granted the night games, extra time-outs, and preoccupation with bowl games, but there was a time when basketball, football, and baseball were very different from the way they are now.

14 A Sporting Proposal

What is the difference between a game and a sport? Are they the same? Are all games sports? No, hopscotch and checkers are not sports; they are games.

But it is true that games such as baseball, basketball, football, and soccer are considered sports. Maybe sports have spectators, and games don't necessarily have spectators, although they may have them. Checkers players may or may not wish to have spectators watching their moves, for example.

Can you take a game and turn it into a sport? That is, can you take games such as hopscotch or jump rope and turn them into spectator sports, as has been done with BMX bike racing and other recreational activities that originally didn't involve announcers, spectators, and prizes? What game would you like to see turned into a sport? Considering what is taking place nowadays in the field of athletic competition, what game offers the most promise for expansion into a sport that would attract spectators and even television coverage? Describe what has to be done to expand the game. If you can, illustrate your ideas with drawings, graphs, and tables.

15
Dogtown

Personifying Dogs

Overview of the Unit

The basic idea of this unit is the rather trite one of personifying animals. In a far more direct way than Jonathan Swift did in *Gulliver's Travels*, we hope to encourage your students to discover various aspects of human nature in portraying dogs as civil servants. Your students are to assign different breeds of dogs to municipal jobs and then draw one of the canine workers, providing it with an appropriate hat.

Idea: Comparing Dogs and Humans Is Revealing

Perhaps the triteness of this exercise in making comparisons between canines and humans won't put off your students. There is an attempt on our part to modify the usual observation of how similar dogs are to their masters and mistresses by asking the student to give dogs human vocations. The justification for this unit resides mainly in the invitation to draw the canine jobholders. Your students deserve a little relief from the usual writing that is required in this and other curricular materials.

Creative Thinking Skill to Be Developed: Enjoying and Using Fantasy

One of the most popular ways to fantasize in an approved way in school is by personifying animals. It's such a popular pastime that personified animals such as Roadrunner and Mickey Mouse are important characters in our culture. Since human beings tend to anthropomorphize animals anyway, and since your students have been exposed to this practice since birth, this unit will not stretch their minds as much as other units. Nevertheless, they will have to do some thinking before coming up with the appropriate breed of dog to be chief air traffic control officer or city manager or judge. Some choices will be nearly automatic but not necessarily reasonable when you consider the breed's characteristics, as in the cases of dalmatian for fire chief and German shepherd for police chief. Which dog would make the best librarian? Maybe your students will have some fun deciding. (We have steered clear of commissioner of water works and supervisor of street cleaning.)

Preparing for the Unit

Any mention of personification, either inside or outside of the curriculum, is all that is needed to warm up your students for this unit. Ideally, an author of a textbook will indulge in this literary device, and you will have a chance to note that weakness, then you can go on to a remark or two about dogs resembling their owners or dogs taking on the personalities or quirks of their owners. (The former tendency has been well documented by photographers, but the latter is perhaps open to debate.)

Presenting the Unit

Except for drawing a mayoral pooch, or whatever role a student chooses for his subject, the unit shouldn't require a great deal of your students' time. On the other hand, "Dogtown" might be the kind of unit that you would like to have your students ponder, so giving it to them to take home and complete might be a good plan. Whatever you decide, this activity is the kind that works well when your class is studying civic government or when your students are in need of a break from the standard assignment.

15 Dogtown

1 The idea of having communities of dogs that carry out the roles of humans is not a new one. A number of artists have depicted animals, principally dogs, acting like humans. Most of these depictions are humorous, of course. There have been other attempts to have animals behave like human beings, from Peter Rabbit to Porky Pig, in stories, cartoons, and fables. The creators of these characters choose their animal characters wisely for the most part, but occasionally an animal is given human characteristics that aren't in keeping with its true nature.

Think about each of the ten community jobs listed below. Then think about the many breeds of dogs that there are, with their varying sizes, dispositions, and capabilities. You can look in any encyclopedia or large dictionary for pictures and descriptions of domesticated dogs. What breed of dog would be well suited to be

Mayor?

Police chief?

Fire chief?

Head librarian?

Director of the electric utility?

City manager?

Principal of the high school?

Coach of the football team?

Chief air traffic control officer at the airport?

Judge?

2 If you have a dog, would your dog be suited for any one of those jobs?
If so, why?

3 Draw a picture of one of those canine jobholders and give it an appropriate hat.

Impossible!

Explaining Incongruities

Overview of the Unit

This unit requires your students to interpret the beginning of another student's story about the future. The story starts off with several incongruities, and your students are asked to explain them. It should challenge their imaginations to come up with rational explanations for the four strange details.

Idea: What at First Seems Implausible Can Turn Out to Make Sense

Withholding judgment until sufficient evidence is obtained is a good policy for everyone, including the teacher portrayed in this unit. At first sight, or first hearing, what is really reasonable can seem incongruous.

Creative Thinking Skill to Be Developed: Looking from a Different Perspective

The teacher depicted in the unit illustrates the personal characteristic opposite from that of one who wants to encourage creative thinking, that is, the suspension of judgment. At first glance, the student (Andre) has included some nonsensical details in his story, namely, February 30, a reckoning of time indicated by 13:12, a three-dollar bill, and change for the bill coming to "five crisp new bills." It requires a little imagination to figure out how you can get "five crisp new bills" in change after paying with a three-dollar bill. (If the bills are of the one-dollar denomination, it would seem that "Billy" is getting a bonus—but why?) We'll wager that most of your students can come up with an explanation. There are explanations, but we won't spoil the fun by revealing them here. (One or two are not so surprising.)

Looking from a different perspective is the creative skill featured in this unit. Your students must interpret the words in the story in such a way that they make sense. This means that "February 30" is somehow legitimate even though there is no such date on our present calendar. If your students recognize that the story takes place 30 years from now and that the setting is not identified at the beginning of the story, they can come up with a rationale for the February 30 date and the other incongruities.

Preparing for the Unit

"Impossible!" makes a couple of points, one being that what might seem ridiculous upon first encounter may turn out to be entirely reasonable. You could use this unit to make that point when your students are quick to jump to conclusions and to make judgments. Any occasion when behavior of that sort is exhibited would be a good time to administer the unit.

You can heighten anticipation in presenting the unit to your students by tossing out the old cliché "Nothing is impossible" and adding, "Isn't that right?" As a matter of fact, we have some difficulty accepting that bromide, and you might get similar expressions of skepticism. Following up the discussion of impossibilities, you can offer this unit and ask your students to judge for themselves whether the teacher in the anecdote is correct.

Presenting the Unit

It is advisable for you to have your students undertake this unit individually and to have a discussion take place after all of them have completed it. The warm-up, per se, takes place when you introduce the unit. In most cases, further warm-up is unnecessary.

The way to produce plausible explanations for the incongruities in Andre's story is to create little scenarios that allow the troublesome details to seem fairly reasonable. For example, why would there be a three-dollar bill thirty years from now? Would inflation have anything to do with it? How long will our present denominations of one-, two-, five-, and ten-dollar bills last? Is there a good reason why there should never be a three-dollar bill? There can be good explanations.

16 Impossible!

A half-hour after he'd asked his students to start writing, Mr. Burroughs was roaming the aisles to see how they were doing. Looking over Andre's shoulder, the teacher paused and frowned. Andre didn't stop writing, however, until Mr. Burroughs exclaimed, "Impossible! Impossible!"

This is what Mr. Burroughs had read when the two words escaped from his mouth:

"It was 13:12 on February 30 when Billy flew the nine miles across town to the youth center. Not much traffic. He alighted at 13:19. Today he'd have to pay for the intergalactic simulation, and so he handed the lady at the entrance his three-dollar bill. She gave him back five crisp new bills."

That was as far as Mr. Burroughs had read. His face wore expressions of outrage and perplexity as he said to his young student: "That's just nonsense, Andre! Explain how all of that makes any sense at all. This was supposed to be an exercise in writing about life thirty years from now, but you have incorporated a lot of ridiculous details in your story."

How can Andre explain those "impossible" details? Andre does have a sound explanation for everything he wrote. What do you think he will tell his teacher?

Facing the Issues © 1994 Zephyr Press, Tucson, Arizona

═══ **17** ═══

Blame

Examining Alibis and Responsibilities

Overview of the Unit

Since it is often good for our egos, if not for our consciences, excusing our mistakes and inadequacies by blaming others is popular the world round. Blaming, the subject of this unit, should ring a few bells. If it doesn't, something is wrong somewhere. We all have a tendency to look elsewhere—to a familiar scapegoat, friend, authority figure, or even loved one—when finding reasons for things going wrong. In this unit we offer a few examples of common blaming and then make it more personal by asking your students if they can endorse any of the six statements that put the blame on other people and things. We finish the unit by having your students consider two technological developments that may make alibiing more difficult in the future.

Idea: Blaming Others and Not Taking Responsibility for One's Actions Only Hurt the Individual

Very few lessons in life are more important to learn than this one, and the earlier a person learns it the better off she or he is. A lifelong habit of alibiing and blaming others can be crippling socially, professionally, and spiritually.

Creative Thinking Skill to Be Developed: Seeing Relationships

Seeing relationships is the general skill to be developed in this unit. The final part asks your students to look for some consequences of the development of two communication technologies. We don't ask for a particular number of consequences for alibiers, but your students should be able to see several if they can imagine how these technologies can be used widely.

Preparing for the Unit

Finding an opportunity for introducing the unit shouldn't be difficult. Young people become fairly adept quite early in their lives at sidestepping responsibility and projecting blame on others. Generally speaking, the more pressure placed upon them, the more likely they are to revert to blaming others. The number of such alibis in a group is probably a good way to gauge the level of pressure placed on the group. When a team loses or when someone complains that it wasn't his or her fault, you can administer "Blame" with just a few words of explanation.

Presenting the Unit

This unit has its basis in psychology, but it ends by asking your students to predict the consequences of two technologies in the field of communications. Thus, we are merging two curricular areas. If you think about it, however, it is very difficult to remove the human, or psychological, element in any discussion of the future. In fact, it is hard to remove the human element in any academic undertaking, even mathematics.

The introduction at the beginning of the unit should be long enough for your students to see the relevance of the topic to their own lives. If they don't, the six statements about avoiding responsibility are designed to hit home. The fifth statement about not being chosen because a couple of people "have it in" for the student, however, could be legitimate and not be an alibi for someone. If you have a discussion of this section of the unit, that statement might get some attention.

In the final section, we invite your students to learn more about two technological developments and how they may make the incidence of blaming others less frequent. Some genuine thinking is called for in this part of the unit; your students won't merely be able to toss out some opinions.

17 Blame

1 A lot of blaming goes on in sports. Fans are quick to blame referees for the losses of their football and basketball teams. There have been riots in some countries when officials have made unpopular decisions in soccer matches. More than one coach has been fired because he "couldn't get along with his players" and the players revolted. The coach sometimes blames the players when games are lost, and the players blame the coach for his insensitivity and outmoded coaching methods.

The examples cited above are of the two-party variety of blaming, but there are literally countless examples of one-party blaming. You can see it in all kinds of situations—the card player who says he made a stupid mistake because the telephone rang in another room; the clumsy oaf who blames his house for being too small when he bangs into doorways and furniture. It's almost a national pastime, this blaming business.

Are any of the following excuses justifiable?

You do poorly on a test because the teacher threw in questions about material not gone over in class.

You get cookie crumbs all over the floor because the cookies weren't baked right.

You can't remember people's names when they are introduced to you because you are occupied with making good eye contact with them.

You don't eat all of those vegetables and foods that are supposed to make you healthy because they taste terrible.

Because a couple of people have it in for you, they saw to it that you weren't chosen.

If people would just stop telling you what to do, you could manage your affairs very well—it's their bossing you that confuses and riles you and causes you to do the wrong things.

If you answered yes to more than one question, you might qualify for the "Alibi Ike Club." People in that club can find a lot of reasons for their mistakes, failures, gaffes, and oversights.

2 Human nature being what it is, we doubt that people will stop blaming others for conditions and events that they don't like. Or is it possible that advances in communication technology will give people fewer opportunities for alibis? How could developments such as these make blaming and excuse-making less frequent in the future?

Development 1: A microchip has been developed that is stunningly quick at recognizing handwriting, identifying military targets, and performing other tasks. Because they can recognize visual or sound patterns at high speed, neural nets are being applied to tricky tasks such as distinguishing human voices, fingerprints, and zip codes.

How can this development reduce blaming and excuse-making?

Facing the Issues © 1994 Zephyr Press, Tucson, Arizona

Development 2: In Personal Communication Service, microwave frequencies are allocated for roaming telephone numbers that follow customers of the service wherever they go.

How can this development reduce blaming and excuse-making?

18
Paradoxically Speaking

Considering the Greenhouse Effect

Overview of the Unit

This might have been an unusual activity ten or twelve years ago, but nowadays there are lots of remarks about oxymorons, and so the concept will probably be familiar to your students. Actually, what we have given in this unit are paradoxical sentences, as the title indicates. An oxymoron is a paradoxical expression, and so there is little difference between this activity and one in which students are asked to translate expressions such as "brilliantly dull" and "cowardly hero."

After an introduction emphasizing that people often utter contradictory statements and questions, your students are asked to explain seven such sentences. Having struggled to make sense of those paradoxical statements and questions, they are then invited to explain how the Earth could be warming and cooling at the same time.

Idea: The Greenhouse Effect Is a Paradox

The greenhouse effect and global warming constitute the curricular focus of this unit. It is quite likely your students will have heard and read a great deal about possible atmospheric changes that can affect their lives and the lives of their children.

The chemical content of the troposphere and stratosphere is a crucial factor in determining the Earth's average temperature and therefore its climates. Carbon dioxide, water vapor, and trace elements of ozone, methane, nitrous oxide, and chlorofluorocarbons play a key role in regulating the temperature. These gases are known as the greenhouse gases, and they act like a pane of glass in a greenhouse that lets in visible light from the sun but prevents some of the heat from escaping back into space. Instead, the heat is radiated back toward the Earth's surface, resulting in a buildup of heat that raises the temperature of the air in the troposphere.

Creative Thinking Skill to Be Developed: Looking from a Different Perspective

Abraham Maslow (1954) notes that the great artist is one who can put together clashing colors and conflicting forms. This ability to reconcile opposites is also the mark of the great statesman, the great inventor, and the great philosopher. These people bring together into harmonious wholes what appear to be opposing elements; they are integrators and unifiers. It may be said that such people are great because they have a larger vision of life than other people have. In "Paradoxically Speaking" we attempt to encourage your students to look at ideas from more than one angle by having them try to make contradictory statements into sensible ones. We call this process the reconciling of opposites, and the creative thinking skill is looking from a different perspective.

Preparing for the Unit

The task of making the contradictory sentences seem reasonable is actually a story-making activity. The student must say to her- or himself, "Oh, yeah, I remember the time I had to wait and wait for dinner, and by the time we finally ate I felt a little sick and almost didn't want to eat." We won't try to explain the other six sentences, but they really can be made to make sense.

The last part of the unit is a good deal more challenging than the seven paradoxical sentences. Would it be possible for the Earth to cool down and warm up at the same time? To respond adequately, your students will need to do some thinking, and they will probably have to do some research. Simultaneous warming and cooling may be possible, but to date no scientists have predicted that trend.

Following through with the Unit

Since it is relatively easy to come up with paradoxical sentences, you may want to present an activity similar to "Paradoxically Speaking" a week or so after your students have encountered this unit. There may be several interesting changes in the way they react the second time around. If the seven sentences in "Paradoxically Speaking" seem unpromising or unsatisfactory, here are others that may be substituted for them. (Or, even better, you may wish to substitute your own sentences for ours.)

By hunting deer and elk, I demonstrate my respect for nature and for wildlife.

If we had more laws, fewer people would be convicted of crimes.

I've come to the conclusion that athletics isn't for athletes.

Why was she chosen when there were three or four people almost as good?

I believe Beethoven wrote his greatest works after he was deaf because he couldn't hear them.

Wakefulness can lead to increased sleep.

Since we spent too much money and went over our budget, let's go out and splurge.

Reference

Maslow, Abraham. 1954. *Motivation and Personality.* New York: Harper and Row.

18 Paradoxically Speaking

1 A man once said to his neighbor, "It wasn't nearly so hot this past summer as expected, but then no one thought it would be." If you don't look at his words too carefully, they aren't so contradictory. What he meant was that weather forecasters (probably some distance away from where he lived) had predicted very hot weather, but most of the local people doubted it would turn out to be  that hot. Many people toss a seemingly contradictory statement into their conversation now and then. Usually the listeners have a good idea of what the speakers mean.

Here are some apparently contradictory statements and questions. Tell what the speakers of these paradoxical sentences really had in mind.

Those were awfully big small pancakes.

The louder he plays the harder it is for me to hear him.

Can I come over and see you after you've gone?

I could eat a lot more if I weren't so hungry.

It would do my old eyes good if you'd just stop talking!

If he loses any more money he'll be wealthy.

Why work for him and get big wages when you can work for me for peanuts?

2 A great many scientists have predicted a decided warming of the Earth's atmosphere and a gradual global warming, but there are other scientists who claim the planet is getting colder. It will probably be one or the other, and in fifty years we'll know who is correct. Or perhaps the situation of predicting global warming or cooling is similar to the statements above. Let's see, that would be: The Earth will warm up and be colder. Can both scientific opinions be right? How could that be?

19

Home Base

Examining Mobility in Our Society

Overview of the Unit

The proposition that is presented to the student in this unit is that people are "pulling up roots" and moving with ever-increasing frequency. Sudden moves, frequent moves, and unexpected moves all can adversely affect the members of a family. Chances are that many of your students have experienced a disruptive move of one kind or another.

Five questions constitute the second section of the unit. Each of the questions deals with the effects on young people that not having a permanent anchor can have. Again, many of your students can speak from experience about the disadvantages and advantages of frequent moves. (One young lady bravely said that she liked to move because then she could make new friends.)

The third section of the unit encourages the student to investigate and then suggest measures that might be taken to reduce the adverse effects of frequent moves in the twenty-first century.

Idea and Issue: Extreme Mobility in Our Society Is Disrupting American Family Life

Mobility translates to disruption for many families, and it is becoming recognized as a contributing factor in the general "breakdown" of the American family. Many sociologists think that too much mobility can accelerate the disintegration of families these days. Since mobility arises from many causes, from people fleeing crime-infested neighborhoods to wage earners being transferred, it is perhaps an exaggeration to say that there is an issue in the United States regarding an increase in mobility. When people move often and against their will, however, there is an issue to be addressed.

The Creative Thinking Skill to Be Developed: Being Sensitive and Aware

Certain young people have the gift of being sensitive to the desires and feelings of others. It would seem that the gift is part of their makeup, a "natural" ability that is part of their personality. Others of us are embarrassed to discover that we often have to be made aware of the plight of someone because we have been honestly unaware of his or her situation or feelings.

At one time the struggle to make people more aware of certain problems in human relationships was termed "consciousness raising." It is that type of activity for which this unit calls. The creative thinking skill, sensitivity and awareness, applies to the entire range of human experience.

Preparing for the Unit

Opportunities for introducing "Home Base" can present themselves when a new student joins a class, when a student leaves the school, when there is a discussion of housing problems (including community problems with the homeless), migrant workers, and so on. It may not be necessary for you to do much warming up in administering this activity to your students except to refer to an occasion when a family has recently moved. A spontaneous discussion may arise that will lead your students into thinking a little more deeply about one of the serious problems of a highly mobile society.

Presenting the Unit

Although the unit begins with an exploration of anchor points for animals, it swiftly moves to that concept in human terms. Regrettably, there is little or no humor in this unit. The topic is a serious one, and so there will be no need for you to underscore the seriousness or importance of the problems of the homeless and the displaced persons in other countries. (The world probably has more displaced persons now than it has had in a very long time.)

You might encourage your pupils to discuss in small groups the problems of moving frequently (or unwillingly). You might use the brainstorming technique. The major rules for brainstorming follow:

1. The more ideas, the better. Wild ideas are encouraged.

2. Criticism is out. Evaluation is deferred until all of the group's ideas are expressed.

3. "Hitchhiking" upon someone else's idea is encouraged.

4. Someone is designated to record the ideas in the order in which they are expressed.

5. Criteria are devised for evaluating all of the ideas, and then the group determines which are the best or most promising.

19　Home Base

1　What is it like to wake up one morning and not know where you are? Does this happen to truck drivers? People who move often or travel constantly suffer because they don't have "anchor points," places that are very familiar to them where they can go.

Each of us, in fact, needs a number of anchor points or bases that we can touch fairly often. If you have been observant, you know that pets and other animals have this same need for places they can go to regularly in order to keep their sense of place. For example, roosters have a favorite perch to which they return regularly during the day. Maybe you can remember some places where these animals go to "touch base":

rabbit

blackbird

squirrel

cat

horse

dog

Facing the Issues © 1994 Zephyr Press, Tucson, Arizona

2 If people move even more often in the twenty-first century than they do now—and it is estimated that the average American family moves every three years—how will people react to having such a transitory home base? How will not having a permanent home base affect

pre-school children?

children in elementary school?

children who are taught at home?

young people who are physically handicapped?

young people who are mentally handicapped?

Home Base *(continued)*

3 What steps might be taken to lessen the harmful effects of moving so often?

20
Put It in Reverse

Examining Reversals

Overview of the Unit

An introductory paragraph leads into an activity in which your students are asked to explain why ten things can or cannot be reversed. The items range from gaining weight to frying an egg. Then students are asked to reverse seven phenomena that have social implications. The unit is one dealing with a concept, reversal, and we hope that your students will find it a fascinating one.

Idea: Some Things Can Be Reversed and Some Can't

The problems of vandalism, employee crime, illiteracy, and the scarcity of landfills are raised in the last section of the unit, and some interesting discussions should arise from conscientiously examining these issues, but the vehicle for the unit is simply applying the reversal concept to a wide variety of situations. In other words, this is an intellectual exercise.

Creative Thinking Skills to Be Developed: Being Sensitive and Aware; Looking from a Different Perspective

Adults are constantly amazed at the details children notice that go unobserved by adults. Young people "see life afresh." Not having become accustomed or habituated to all of the phenomena that adults take for granted or ignore, children find enjoyment and excitement in discovering these phenomena. It is that kind of freshness of seeing things anew that can be brought about by thinking about why some things can be done and undone (shoe laces), other things can be placed and replaced (employees) or built up and torn down (buildings), and some things can be started and reversed (a movie projector). Looking at different processes as reversible or irreversible is akin to "looking at life with new eyes." From that perspective, the student can be led to understand that on this planet there are processes, such as aging, that are fundamentally different from a rise in the crime rate. Some things can—and should—be reversed.

Preparing for the Unit

The serious part of the unit is found in the last section, which deals with crime, blood pressure, illiteracy, physical debilitation, and the scarcity of landfills for society's garbage. If any of those topics arises naturally in a discussion, you will have an excellent opportunity to introduce this unit. The unit will also serve well in the event you want to use it to kick off one of those topics for study.

Presenting the Unit

In all probability you will find that "Put It in Reverse" needs a discussion at the end of the first activity or when you complete the unit. As in most discussions, some young people will make certain observations that are worth sharing with their fellow students. We are convinced of the importance of students learning from one another as well as from their teachers and textbooks. If the unit accomplishes what we intend it to, a number of interesting insights about reversibility and society will be gained by your students.

20 Put It in Reverse

1 There are times when we fervently wish we could reverse a process, such as aging or slipping into a bad habit. Some processes can be reversed, of course; cars, movies, and tape recordings can be reversed (English in reverse sounds a lot like Norwegian, interestingly enough). But it is impossible to turn many events around and have them occur in the opposite order in which they happened. The familiar science fiction notion of a time machine taking people back in time is not, literally speaking, reversing the events of history. The time travelers are just transported back, all at once, to a former time.

Reversing outcomes is a relatively common kind of reversal. In basketball, for example, one referee can say Team A gets the ball out of bounds, but he or she can be overruled by the other two officials, and the decision can be made to give it to Team B.

Explain why the following events can or cannot be reversed:

A football player carrying a ball and heading laterally across the field

Building a brick wall

Frying an egg in a pan

The direction of the wind

Put It in Reverse *(continued)*

Acquiring wealth

The stance of a politician about an issue such as public funds for private schools

Learning to read

Gaining weight

Writing a letter

Building a friendship

2 How would you reverse the following?

The "graying" of white clothes

A rise in blood pressure readings

Decreasing strength in the legs

A rise in illiteracy

The increase of vandalism throughout the country

The increasing scarcity of sites for dumping garbage

The increase in employee crime

21
Disappearing Snowflakes

Making Analogies of the Weather

Overview of the Unit

This unit is comprised of a discussion of the significance of snowflakes in one's life, four questions concerning the weather as a metaphor for human conditions, and a question about whether there ever will be a situation in which people aren't concerned with the weather. In contemplating different aspects of weather, your students are led from the here and now of their world to some metaphorical comparisons to the unknown realm of the future.

Idea: There Are Parallels between the Weather and Human Affairs

We describe arguments between people as stormy scenes, and agreeable individuals are referred to as having sunny dispositions. Analogies featuring various aspects of the weather are commonplace.

Creative Thinking Skill to Be Developed: Looking from a Different Perspective

Analogizing is a popular technique among those individuals who deliberately try to foster creative thinking in others. It is also a familiar literary device. In this unit it is used to cause your students to see human affairs from different perspectives. For some individuals, comparing the forces and phenomena of nature to human affairs is second nature. For others—

often those who tend to look at things in an unimaginative, matter-of-fact way—making analogies of the sort proposed in this unit verges on the preposterous. As you know, some of your best students are found in the second category. They are the ones who can benefit most from an activity such as the analogizing in this unit.

Preparing the Unit

Since the weather is nearly always a topic of speculation, this unit can fit in during any time of the school year, although it probably would have more relevance in the winter. One obvious occasion for using it is after a snowfall (providing snow does fall in your region). When the temperature hovers around 34°F, snowflakes usually melt on pavement and fail to accumulate on grass and plants. If your students have had much experience with snow, they won't have to be reminded of "disappearing snowflakes."

Presenting the Unit

This is perhaps one of those units that doesn't require much open discussion after the initial warm-up, which can come shortly after you make a comment concerning the weather. The analogizing, to be at all effective in developing the looking-from-a-different-perspective skill, should be done privately by the students. After the unit is completed by all of your students, you can conduct a discussion about the analogies and about future environments with controlled atmospheric conditions, with the entire class chiming in.

21 Disappearing Snowflakes

1 When you see snowflakes, what do you think of? Beauty? Movement? Change? Danger? All of those thoughts—and more—come into the minds of people who see snow falling. In some places it can mean a day off from school and sledding for some and skiing over the week-end for others. There are places where it can mean traffic jams and a miserable commute to work. In yet other places it can mean "just another winter day."

That the weather is changeable in most areas of the world can't be denied. A downpour of rain, a thunderstorm, sleet, hail, and other skies can be likened to the events in the lives of people. In fact, one of our best known sayings is an analogy of the weather and the vicissitudes of life: "It never rains but it pours."

Following are some questions about different kinds of weather.

2 Respond to the following questions:

What in world affairs is like snowflakes falling at 33°F and not "sticking" and melting on the ground?

What in world affairs is like six feet of snow falling overnight?

Facing the Issues © 1994 Zephyr Press, Tucson, Arizona

What in world affairs is like snow falling the day after the sun had melted the snow on the streets and it had turned to ice overnight?

What in world affairs is like snow mixed with freezing rain?

3 Will there ever be a time when people don't have to worry about the weather? What kinds of environments could people find themselves in where the weather does not play an important part in their lives?

22
Praying Rats

Taking a Different Look at Genetic Engineering

Overview of the Unit

This unit starts off with a somewhat ridiculous and patently illogical proposition, namely, that because detectives are like hawks and also like cats, hawks are therefore similar to cats. Of course, they do share some behavior traits and anatomical characteristics—quite a few, in fact. Three more illogical conclusions are drawn in a similar manner, and for all four pairings your students are asked to show similarities between the animals. The matter of genetic engineering is then introduced, and your students are to think of the animal whose genes might be most popular in gene splicing experiments of the future.

Idea: Genetic Engineering Can Be Beneficial or Harmful to Humanity and Nature

Genetic engineering, according to some scientists, can be very dangerous. A controversy has been raging about the benefits and dangers of genetic engineering ever since it became commonly known that the technique of gene splicing existed. Now there is an entire industry that is founded on the technique. We predict that there will continue to be concerns expressed about genetic engineering for decades to come.

Creative Thinking Skill to Be Developed: Looking from a Different Perspective

If you examine an object from various perspectives—from above, below, inside, and so on—you obtain different sets of information. (The well-known fable of the blind men and the elephant illustrates the point best.) In like fashion, you can examine natural phenomena from a multitude of perspectives. It follows, then, that if you examine any living thing and compare it with another living thing, you can find features that the two organisms have in common.

The creative thinking skill of being able to see events, ideas, inanimate objects, people and other living things, processes, institutions, and so on, from several points of view is invaluable to inventors, painters, sculptors, writers, musicians, dress designers, architects, comedians, and industrial engineers, among others. Straight-line thinking and perceiving are anathema to the production of original ideas.

Preparing for the Unit

The unit can be associated with the curricular area of biology, naturally enough. It also has a direct relationship with critical thinking and logic. Accordingly, when genetic engineering, fallacious reasoning, or classifying animals is being discussed, "Praying Rats" can be introduced. Admittedly, the unit runs somewhat contrary to the orderly approach of the biological sciences. Nevertheless, you can make a point or two about the kinship of all living things on earth.

Presenting the Unit

Depending upon the sophistication of your students in dealing with syllogisms and challenging fallacious arguments, you may or may not want to go over the first part of the unit with them before they tackle the unit individually. We don't anticipate that your students will be stumped when asked to find similarities between the rat and the praying mantis, the dog and the penguin, cats and hawks, or eels and bears. (An answer can be as simple as: "They are both found on this planet.") A discussion about the similarities of the cat and the hawk should give your students enough clues to come up with answers for the other analogies.

The final section, in which your students are to predict what animal will become the most popular in experiments involving gene splicing, is a different matter. Some of your students won't have much information upon which to make a prediction, and so you should encourage them to get the information they need to make an intelligent prediction. We hope that there also will be individuals in your class who question the gene splicing on ethical grounds. The ethical problems of genetic engineering haven't been resolved as yet, nor are they likely to be resolved soon.

22 Praying Rats

1 Detectives and hawks are alike because they both have keen eyesight. Detectives are also like cats because they can be very still and quiet when stalking their prey. If detectives are like hawks and also like cats, does that mean that hawks and cats are alike? The rules of logic might deny that there is a similarity between cats and hawks, but of course, they <u>are</u> similar. In what ways are they similar?

2 Let's try a couple more analogies.

Wolves and rats are both mammals. Wolves and praying mantises are predators. Therefore, rats must be like praying mantises. In what ways are rats like praying mantises?

Otters and dogs can both be playful. Otters and penguins are more graceful and swifter in the water than on land. Accordingly, dogs and penguins are similar (in violation of the rules of logic). How are dogs and penguins alike?

Let's have a go at even one more. Lizards are like eels because they both have two eyes. Lizards and bears both have tails. Therefore eels and bears, contrary to the rules of logic, must be alike in some way. In what ways are eels and bears alike?

Facing the Issues © 1994 Zephyr Press, Tucson, Arizona

3 Animals can be given the characteristics of other animals by means of genetic engineering. It is possible to give the traits of one animal to another when scientists utilize gene-splicing techniques. In the future, sheep might be given one or more traits of a goat so that sheep might be a little more intelligent. A good deal of genetic engineering has already been done with plants, and a little has been done with animals. Which do you predict will be the animal species whose genes will most often be "borrowed" to alter the characteristic of other animals? That is, which animal will have its genes transferred most often?

Why do you think that will be so?

23

Joy

Examining Differences in Joyful Experiences

Overview of the Unit

We're not sure that this unit will be enjoyable for your students, but it could be a relief from their studying about wars, corruption, pollution, and crime. After a brief discussion about the transitory nature of joy we ask them to recall ten situations and think about how enduring their feelings of joy were in those situations. Then there is a personal question concerning the particular joy that lasts longest for the student. Finally, we present four scenes and ask how much joy various individuals receive from their experiences.

Idea: Life Is Full of Joy

Since unit 13 is about pain, it might be effective to have this unit follow it closely in time, or vice versa. Which unit would you present first? The strategic and psychological choices could be to have joy follow pain, but that is not the way it usually works, or is it? It seems to be that way in childbirth and long-distance running, however.

Creative Thinking Skills to Be Developed:
Being Aware of Emotions; Looking from a Different Perspective

In *Making the Creative Leap Beyond* (1993), E. Paul Torrance makes a case for regarding the ability to be aware of emotions in oneself and others as an important element in creative production. He states, "There is now relatively widespread acceptance of the idea that emotional, nonrational, and suprarational factors are more important in creative thinking than purely cognitive, rational factors." This unit is designed to sensitize your students to the fact that there are more than just bittersweet experiences. There are all kinds of joy, and often they are mixed up for the person involved in a joyous experience.

Preparing for the Unit

There will be occasions when you will find that the majority of your students appear to be insensitive to the views or predicaments of groups of people. At such times this unit can be administered with the hope that they will see more than one side of local, national, and international disputes. Although schools don't eradicate prejudices and misconceptions, they are institutions that allow people of different backgrounds to mix and to become aware of religious, ethnic, social, and economic differences.

Presenting the Unit

It might be a good plan to have a general discussion of the first two sections of "Joy" with your students and then to put them on their own in the third section. After they have all had a chance to react to the four scenes individually, you can hold another discussion regarding their views of the emotions evoked in the four situations.

Although it may appear that there is a bit too much of the psychological in this unit, we believe that at least one of the situations will hit home for a majority of your students and lead them to have an insight or two about how people react emotionally to experiences.

Reference

Torrance, E. Paul, and H. Tammy Safter. 1993. *Making the Creative Leap Beyond.* Buffalo, N.Y.: Bearly Limited.

23 Joy

1 We have a few words that are as important as, or more important than, any words in our language. One is love. Another is joy. The invitation "Enjoy!" is a cliche as much as "Have a good day" is, but just to say a word that has "joy" in it gives most of us pleasure. The trouble is that joy doesn't seem to last long enough, as happens when your team wins and everyone on your side is elated, but the joy doesn't quite last until the next game.

How long does your joy last after the following occasions?

After getting the right answer during a class discussion

After being told you are going to get your favorite dessert

After getting a good grade

After finding money on the sidewalk or in a parking lot

After getting the present you wanted for your birthday

After beating another person in a game

After being told that you have won a contest

After getting out of school for summer vacation

After winning a bet with someone

After doing someone a favor

2 What joy lasts longest for you?

Why?

3 Following are four scenes. Tell whether you think the people involved in the situations derive joy from the events.

After several years of trying, a girl finally gets the chance to be a member of the cast in the big school pageant, which comes each year at the end of May. She is given a minor role. The girl rushes home to tell her parents. What does she feel?

A young man applies for a job at a warehouse. His father has been unemployed for seventeen months, and his mother doesn't make quite enough money to pay the family's bills. The interviewer seems a little hesitant, but he finally says: "Okay, show up tomorrow at eight sharp. You have the job." What emotions does the young man have?

What are the emotions of the interviewer?

Facing the Issues © 1994 Zephyr Press, Tucson, Arizona

A sixteen-year old boy fails the written examination for his driver's license. After a good deal of studying, he passes the written exam, but then he fails the road test. He turns to the left from the right-hand lane, and the examiner informs him that he must take the test again. A week later, he passes the road test and his picture is taken for his license. What emotions does he feel as his photograph is taken?

An angry basketball coach yells at his players during a time-out when they are four points ahead because they had been twelve points ahead a few minutes earlier. The team wins by one point. Does the coach have a sense of joy at the game's end? What other emotions might he have?

What emotions do his players have?

24

Fifty Years from Now

Making Predictions about Future Modes of Transportation

Overview of the Unit

The topic of this unit is transportation. It has three sections. The first asks several questions about how people got around a hundred years ago, and the second section poses four questions about how people will transport themselves fifty years hence. The unit ends with an invitation to draw the kind of running shoe that might be popular when the student is fifty years older.

Idea: Travel Could Be Quite Different Fifty Years from Now

Transportation is critically important in almost every phase of modern living. What changes will take place in the next fifty years and how will they affect the lives of your students?

Creative Thinking Skill to Be Developed: Being Original

The thinking skill to be developed by engaging in this activity is analogous to the nonverbal type of test item used in a creative thinking test. We have found that type of test item so popular that, after finishing the nonverbal portion of a test battery, students have requested more. Drawing a shoe may or may not be enjoyable for your students, but certainly there is a great deal of emphasis placed upon various kinds of shoes now, thanks largely to the advertising campaigns of the shoe companies.

Preparing for the Unit

If transportation occupies an important part of your social studies curriculum, "Fifty Years from Now" can be introduced at any propitious time. Transportation is so fundamental to nearly everything that goes on in our lives that there should be many occasions for using it. In addition, if a discussion of athletic shoes occurs, either naturally or by your plan, the unit can be even more effective.

Presenting the Unit and Following Through

Unlike some of the units in this book, "Fifty Years from Now" calls for some definite knowledge on the part of your students, at least in the first section. They should be encouraged to get facts about how people transported themselves a hundred years ago if they don't have enough information to answer the questions intelligently.

The second section calls for some knowledge, too, because to predict what the modes of transportation will be like in fifty years requires knowledge of recent developments in the field, plans for future transportation systems, and technological advances. In view of these requirements, we recommend that this unit be administered over a two- or three-day span of time.

A natural outcome of your students' completion of this unit is to arrange a display of the futuristic shoes they have designed. There will probably be some highly imaginative shoes among those submitted by students who are willing to put their creations on display.

This unit has the advantage of appealing to those of your students who are not inspired by assignments to write words and are happier expressing themselves in nonverbal ways.

24 Fifty Years from Now

1

The way we transport ourselves from one place to another has changed greatly since George Washington's day, or even since Teddy Roosevelt's day. It is startling to think that the horse was the everyday mode of transportation for people until the twentieth century. That is, the horse was the main way in which people transported themselves when they didn't walk. Jet lag, the problem that many travelers have when they go from one time zone to another in a day, would have seemed fantastic to someone in Teddy Roosevelt's time.

Will people fifty years from now have problems traveling that we haven't dreamed of yet?

A hundred years ago, instead of taking an airplane to go 5,000 miles, you would have

In a very small town, one hundred years ago, how would you have posted a letter to reach someone 150 miles away if you were in a hurry for it to arrive there?

In New York City, a hundred years ago, you would travel 26 blocks by _____ , instead of taking a cab or the subway.

A hundred years ago, instead of driving a car or riding a motorcycle to travel to a town 40 miles away, you would

How would you have reached a lake in the mountains, where fishing was especially good, from the closest town a hundred years ago?

If you were looking for a "fun ride" in the country a hundred years ago, how would you go?

Facing the Issues © 1994 Zephyr Press, Tucson, Arizona

2 If travel has changed so much in the past hundred years, it may change a great deal in the next fifty years.

Fifty years from now, instead of driving a car or riding a motorcycle to a town 40 miles away, how might you travel?

In Chicago, fifty years from now, how would you travel 26 blocks to reach your destination?

Fifty years from now, how would you travel 5,000 miles?

If you were hoping to have a "fun ride" in the countryside, how would you go?

3 Will people be wearing the same kinds of shoes fifty years from now? What about running shoes? What will they be like? Draw sketches of the shoe that will be most popular for running. Draw one picture from the top view, one from a side view, and one of the bottom (sole). You can use the space below.

Facing the Issues © 1994 Zephyr Press, Tucson, Arizona

$$==25==$$

Good Fences

Examining a Dispute between Neighbors

Overview of the Unit

The unit begins with a summary of the kind of dispute that is unavoidable wherever people live near one another, namely, the financial responsibility for building a fence to separate two properties. Property rights are among the dearest rights of all to some people. There are also a great many people who behave differently from the way they usually do when money enters the picture. The woman and the man in the story are probably not too different from most people in respect to those two traits. We ask your students to side with one party and to give reasons for their partisanship, and then we challenge them to offer a solution to the dispute.

Idea: Good Fences Don't Always Make Good Neighbors

When it comes to personal relationships, it's very difficult for things to go smoothly all of the time.

Creative Thinking Skill to Be Developed: Being Aware of Emotions

As Torrance states in *The Incubation Model of Teaching* (Torrance and Safter 1990), an emphasis upon emotional or nonrational factors will result in higher levels of creative thinking. Instead of having insights imposed upon them, students can deal with subjects through emotional experiences to gain insights. The experiences can be vicarious, as would be the case with "Good Fences," or direct and personal.

Preparing for the Unit

Unfortunately, so many conflicts arise in the lives of most of us that you won't lack for opportunities to tie in a conflict with this unit. Obviously conflicts occur everywhere, including at school and in the community. Disputes between neighbors are common, of course, and it is likely that your students could cite several if you introduce that subject to them. A few words from you about misunderstandings and squabbles should warm up your students sufficiently before they begin reading about Mr. Kimball and Mrs. White.

Presenting the Unit

There is an opportunity in "Good Fences" to have a debate about which party in the dispute is "more correct." (We believe each has a fairly good argument to put forth in his or her behalf.) The nature of the debate can be informal, without following the rules of formal debating. One of the most interesting aspects of such an activity for a teacher is to learn which students line up on the opposing sides.

Role-playing the dispute might also provide your students with insights they might not otherwise obtain. Following are three techniques used in role playing:

Direct Presentation Technique. The students are asked to act out a problem situation, conflict situation, or new situation. Those who are either directly involved in the problem or who are emotionally involved in finding a solution to the problem are usually chosen to do the acting.

Soliloquy Techniques. One actor may engage in a monologue concerning his or her silent, unverbalized reactions in the situation. Or the technique may involve a portrayal by side dialogues and silent actions of hidden thoughts and feelings, parallel with overt thoughts and actions. Soliloquy techniques are especially useful in producing original solutions when thinking is blocked by emotional reactions.

Mirror Technique. In this technique, another actor represents the original actor in the conflict situation, copying his or her behavior patterns and showing "as if in a mirror" how other people perceive the original actor. This technique can help the actor leap emotional blocks to produce better solutions for the conflict situation.

Reference

Torrance, E. Paul, and Tammy Safter. 1990. *The Incubation Model of Teaching.* Buffalo, N.Y.: Bearly Limited.

25 Good Fences

1 The old saying is that "good fences make good neighbors," but after Mr. Kimball had built a fence between his property and Mrs. White's, there was a lot of animosity on both sides of the fence. They squabbled about how much Mrs. White should pay for the fence. She thought she shouldn't pay more than a third of the cost because the fence was Mr. Kimball's idea. She didn't care about having a fence between the two properties (but she hadn't objected when Mr. Kimball proposed that he build the fence). Besides, Mrs. White was in very modest circumstances, or at least that was what she told everybody. Mr. Kimball had his doubts about how poor she was.

Once the fence was built and paid for by Mr. Kimball, an exchange of letters between the two neighbors brought about no resolution of the dispute. Half of the neighborhood sided with Mr. Kimball, and the other half was sympathetic with Mrs. White. Before long there were several arguments in the neighborhood about who was right.

Mrs. White is seventy-two years old and has been a widow for ten years. Mr. Kimball, who just turned sixty-eight, has a wife and two married children. He has recently retired from the railroad with a comfortable pension. They both have many friends in the community and are generally well liked.

What is at stake in this dispute? Name at least three issues.

Good Fences *(continued)*

2 With whom are you inclined to sympathize?

Can you think of the reasons why you would be on that person's side? Do you have any prejudices that might influence you in this matter?

3 What solution can you offer that might resolve the issue and reduce the antipathy between the two parties?

26

¿Qué Hora Es?

Imagining Future Timepieces

Overview of the Unit

This unit starts off with a mundane question and ends with an invitation to make a sketch of a watch, clock, or other timepiece. In between, we ask questions about how timepieces are powered and what kinds of changes will occur in the timekeeping industry in the next twenty years. It really is amazing how electronic inventions have changed the timekeeping business, although your students may be too young to appreciate those changes fully.

Idea: Keeping Track of the Time May Take Some Different Forms in the Future

Some people try to ignore the advance of time, but it is the variable underlying everything in life.

Creative Skills to Be Developed: Being Original; Combining Ideas and Elements

This unit attempts to induce some practical thinking. At least, thinking about technological developments in the field of reckoning time has been a profitable activity for a number of inventors, designers, and manufacturers for some time now. (Excuse us. The word time appears so often in our thinking that it is hard not to come up with unintentional puns when writing about timekeeping.)

It would be very difficult to design a timepiece that didn't have one or two features current timepieces have, so, to an extent, the creative thinking skill to be developed in this unit is one of combining ideas and elements. Those ideas and elements will come together in the student's sketch in ways that may surprise the student her- or himself. This activity is the kind that might appeal to those students who are more mechanically minded and not so fond of playing around with words.

Preparing for and Presenting the Unit

It would seem that this unit can be administered at almost any time in the school day and during any part of the school year. It is written in such a way that you don't have to lead a discussion during the first part. We believe it would be better, however, if you do. If your less able students might be perplexed at all about the questions concerning Molly's clocks, a class discussion is advisable. The first two parts constitute a warm-up for the third and fourth parts of the unit.

The administration of the unit could possibly last more than a class period. On the other hand, those students who aren't motivated by our invitations to think about future timepieces will be finished with the activity in short order. That is so in nearly any activity, of course—some young people take hold and dig in, and others reject the activity or languish.

26   ¿Qué Hora Es?

1   Molly has two clocks in her bedroom. Half of the time they agree—they show the same time. Half of the time they disagree.

What is the reason the clocks aren't always the same?

Fifty years ago the question above about the clocks would have stumped nearly everyone. Why?

2   Molly actually has eight clocks in her house. She doesn't think much about it, but they are powered in three different ways.

What are those three sources of power?

3   It used to be common for people to dial a number and ask for the time on the telephone. The telephone company began to charge for those calls, and the popularity of calling for the time dropped. For those people concerned about the exact time, however, the cable television people have thoughtfully provided the time—hour, minutes, second, AM or PM—along with the weather forecast and announcements on an extra channel.

Facing the Issues © 1994 Zephyr Press, Tucson, Arizona

In the past two decades there have been a number of changes in the ways timepieces are constructed. Since we spend a lot of time keeping track of time in our culture, the timekeeping business is an important one to us, so we can anticipate more developments in the business of letting people know the time. What changes do you envision will occur in that business in twenty years?

What changes can you foresee for the timepiece that is carried on one's person?

What changes do you foresee taking place in determining time in a residence?

What changes do you foresee taking place in the way time will be watched in a place of work?

4 Make a sketch or diagram of one of the timepieces you think might become popular twenty years from now. You'll probably want to incorporate features now present in timepieces with features yet to be used.

=27=
Human Potential

Examining the Notion of Progress

Overview of the Unit

This unit starts off with a discussion of overachievement, and then there is a discussion of the limits of human potential, which leads to seven questions about improvements that can be made in the future in such areas as crime prevention, meteorology, and health. Finally, your students are asked to select one of the improvements they foresee and tell how it will affect them when they are fifty years older.

Idea: The Limits to Human Progress
Are Virtually Unlimited

If human beings are getting bigger and stronger, are they also getting smarter? In this unit we cite technological progress as proof that humans are improving intellectually. Not everyone agrees, however.

Creative Thinking Skill to Be Developed:
Putting Ideas into Context

Although they are only guessing about future improvements, your students will be putting into context their notions about one of tomorrow's gains when they describe an improvement that will change their lives in the future. They don't have to be too specific about the improvement and how it will fit in with the other changes of the future, of course. In *Making the Creative Leap Beyond* (1993), Torrance states that we now "recognize that any one cause may produce any one of many effects, and, further, that any particular effect may be produced by any one of many possible causes or combinations of causes." He goes on to say, "We realize now that these relationships have to be seen in context, that the entire system must be considered."

Preparing for and Presenting the Unit

This unit is another one that covers a lot of intellectual territory. We suggest that you alter its content to accommodate your students' backgrounds and abilities if it seems that our items are inappropriate for them. Different kinds of improvement can be listed in the second section if you can determine what might better "turn them on."

If there is an opportunity, you might want to investigate with your students the idea of "progress." A century ago a majority of Americans were convinced of the inevitability of progress. There are far more people today who are skeptical of the idea. It would be most interesting to learn if your students are optimistic or pessimistic about the directions our society is taking in such areas as quality of life and personal satisfaction.

The last section, which invites your students to predict how an improvement might affect them personally, can be an assignment that is given when the individual student has acquired enough information to respond intelligently. In most cases, that will mean the student will have to do some inquiring, and that would mean research and questioning authorities. Accordingly, the unit should be administered over several days, at a minimum, if your students are to derive much benefit from engaging in it.

Reference

Torrance, E. Paul, and Tammy Safter. 1993. *Making the Creative Leap Beyond.* Buffalo, N.Y.: Bearly Limited.

27 Human Potential

1 The class was having a discussion about scholastic performances, and the words *overachiever* and *underachiever* were used several times. When one student used both terms, the teacher asked her for a definition of the words.

"An underachiever is someone who does less than he or she can do, and an overachiever is someone who does more than he or she can do," she offered.

"That's an interesting idea," the teacher said. "How can anyone do more than he or she can do?"

What do you think?

2 The capacity for improvement in human beings is remarkable. We keep meticulous records of our physical and intellectual achievements to prove it. It is interesting to note that, over the past four decades, the amount of improvement in horse racing times hasn't been as great as it has been in human runners' racing times. Moreover, humans, while physically not as strong as horses, apes, or oxen, are getting bigger and stronger.

What are the limits to human improvement? In physical skills, it is possible that human beings in the past two millennia have been underachieving, but it can't be argued that we humans have been underachieving intellectually—or so it would seem from a review of our technological advances. Nevertheless, there are areas of human endeavor where improvement might come in the next fifty years or so. Predict the improvements that may, or should, come in the next fifty years in these areas:

Hurricane forecasting

Human Potential *(continued)*

Law enforcement and the reduction of crime

Earthquake prediction

Reduction of epidemics

Reduction of malnutrition and starvation

Wars between nations and between groups of people

Stabilization of the world's population

28

The Three Rights

Speculating about the Impact of Personalities upon History

Overview of the Unit

This unit is apparently brief. It doesn't take up a lot of space, and it only consists of an introduction and an activity. Take a closer look at the activity, however, and you can see that there is quite a bit required of your students. The unit starts off with a brief discussion of the old argument about outstanding people influencing their times versus the times creating outstanding individuals. That leads to an exercise of "What Would Have Happened If . . . ?" but with a twist. We name five very famous people in five different fields and ask your students to mix up their dates and homelands. They are invited to speculate about the course of history if Daniel Boone had lived in England in Shakespeare's time, for example, or if Marie Curie had been born in China and not in Poland.

Idea: It Is People Who Direct and Shape the Course of History

What are the nonhuman forces that affect the events of history? Do floods, earthquakes, fires, droughts, sunspots, and hurricanes have as much to do with the course of history as human beings do? These events certainly have direct effects upon the welfare of the earth's inhabitants, human and infra-human.

Creative Thinking Skills to Be Developed: Combining Ideas and Elements; Looking from a Different Perspective

The creative thinking skills to be developed in this unit are complementary. In switching the places and dates of the five famous people, your students will also see events, personalities, forces, and epochs in different lights.

Preparing for the Unit

You may have occasions during a discussion of a historical figure to toss out the idea that perhaps he or she wouldn't have been so outstanding if he or she had been born at a different time and in a different place. This notion isn't new, of course, and it might have even been considered by one or more of your students. The "What Would Have Happened If . . . ?" technique has its limitations, but it has an appeal because it is somewhat off the beaten track and it allows your students to see relationships they might have never seen otherwise.

Presenting the Unit

Because of its nature, this intellectual exercise requires considerable mental effort of your students. It presupposes a knowledge of different periods of history, and students may not have sufficient information to do the hypothesizing about the transposed historical figures. Therefore, you certainly may substitute other persons with whom your students are familiar or have been studying. A comparison of their ideas in a follow-up discussion will reveal how much thinking your students actually did.

28   The Three Rights

More than one person has noted that success in various human endeavors is a matter of timing. Put the right person in the right place at the right time, and it is likely that things will go right. There has been a good deal of speculation as to whether certain political leaders, inventors, and entertainers would have done so well in another era or in another place. Some people argue that it is the total situation that actually "produces" the outstanding individuals; that is to say, the context makes it possible for those individuals to make maximum use of their particular gifts.

Whether or not this line of reasoning is entirely correct is a moot point. We can only wonder that someone like Hitler could come along and take over a nation and almost a continent with his particular traits and talents. In another time, in another country, Hitler might have spent a life in obscurity—or in jail.

Why don't you take the following five individuals and mix them up with each other in terms of when they came into prominence and where they lived? For example, you can exchange the era in which two of the individuals lived. You might also swap the places in which two of these persons gained fame. Or, you can put one person in another's time *and* place. Then, for each of the five, speculate how the individual's history and the history of humanity might have been different.

Individual	Time	Place
Confucius	551–479 B.C.E.	China
Johann Sebastian Bach	1685–1750	Germany
William Shakespeare	1564–1616	England
Daniel Boone	1734–1820	Kentucky and Missouri
Marie S. Curie	1867–1934	France

=29=
Crucial Cooperation

Investigating the Concept of Cooperation

Overview of the Unit

Cooperation as a concept has been taught on television by the Children's Television Workshop through "Sesame Street" since 1971. We are not sure whether or not any change in behavior has resulted from children acquiring the concept of cooperation, but we know from firsthand experience that young children do grasp the concept. In this unit, the idea of *critical* cooperation is presented in the story about the Adèlie penguins, and then your students are asked to draw an analogy between the penguin's cooperation and the world of economics.

Idea: Crucial Cooperation Occurs among Humans as well as among Animals

This unit puts forth the notion that crucial or critical cooperation, that is, cooperation that is necessary to the survival of two individuals or groups of individuals, exists in the world of commerce. The European Economic Community may or may not be a good example of economic cooperation among nations—and it is pushing the analogy to describe the EEC as an example of critical cooperation—but there <u>are</u> examples to be found at other levels.

Creative Thinking Skill to Be Developed: Putting Ideas into Context

One of the most intriguing ways of putting an idea into context is to draw an analogy. William J. J. Gordon (1973) has developed analogizing into a highly effective technique for solving problems in industry. His approach, called synectics, has also been used in the regular classroom. Using synectics, participants do a good deal of playing—they play with words, they play with metaphor, and they play with pushing a fundamental law or basic concept to its limits. Groups using this method of problem solving depend primarily upon these four kinds of metaphor for making the familiar strange and the strange familiar: personal analogy, direct analogy, symbolic analogy, and fantasy analogy.

Torrance (1970) recommends interdisciplinary learning as an effective way of enabling young people to practice putting ideas into context. Gordon (1973) also has found that putting people from entirely different backgrounds in a problem-solving group is the best way to obtain excellent solutions. Cross-age groupings in schools have been popular from time to time, and they offer considerable promise in creative projects and assignments.

Preparing for the Unit

The logical tie-in for this unit is with topics in economics such as management-labor relations, international trade, anti-trust laws, and so on. With so much news about the nations of Europe trying to combine economically in the European Common Market or European Economic Community, there have been many occasions when this unit might have been effectively used in recent years. There probably will be many more occasions in the years to come when cooperation is of critical importance to the survival of industries, communities, and even nations. At this writing, a trade agreement among the United States, Canada, and Mexico is being ratified by the three countries.

Presenting the Unit

Perhaps an analogy such as the one proposed in this unit is more challenging than one, say, of taking an idea such as robotics in the automobile industry and applying it in a somewhat different context such as agribusiness. Not that cooperation in practical economics is rare; it is very common. Sometimes economic cooperation is found in the form of a treaty removing trade barriers between countries; sometimes it is a cartel; and sometimes it is collusion. Bartering of goods and services is a popular form of economic cooperation. The key word used in the title of this unit is *crucial,* that is, when survival of something depends upon co-operation. It is this distinction that we hope your students will see in the expression "critical cooperation."

References

Gordon, W. J. J. 1973. *The Metaphorical Way of Knowing.* Cambridge, Mass.: Synectics Education Systems.

Torrance, E. Paul. 1970. *Encouraging Creativity in the Classroom.* Dubuque, Iowa: William C. Brown.

29 Crucial Cooperation

It has been determined that the major cause of mortality among Adèlie penguins is the tardiness of one parent in relieving the other before and after eggs are laid. Apparently this same problem occurs with other species of penguins. The cooperation of the two parents is crucial during the period just before and after the eggs are hatched. Since both the mother and the father must fast while guarding the nest, one bird cannot remain feeding at sea too long or its mate will be forced to leave the nest because its supply of fat will be used up. A leopard seal will sometimes permanently postpone the return of the adult penguin at sea. When a mate is overdue or lost and the adult guarding the nest leaves it, death for the chicks can ensue because of freezing temperatures and predators such as skuas.

Where in our human society can be found an example of such crucial cooperation? Can you see an analogy in the field of economics? Think about economic arrangements at individual, corporate, national, and international levels, and then show how an arrangement or system similar to that of the penguin parents works.

30
Comings and Goings

Examining Human Migration

Overview of the Unit

This unit is about migrations—comings and goings. After a brief definition of the concept, the student is presented with the idea that people, as well as animals, migrate. (Some biologists speak of plants migrating, as well.) The student is then asked to think about the various events that result in human migration, picking the one most likely to occur in the next decade.

Idea: Human Migrations Are the Result of Small as well as Big Events

Imbedded in the unit's last section is the notion that large movements of people can be caused by seemingly minor events. It will take some imaginative thinking on the part of your students to reconstruct a migration resulting from a wedding, but such a thing could happen—and probably has.

Creative Thinking Skills to Be Developed: Being Sensitive and Aware; Anticipating Consequences

Implicit in the skill of being sensitive and aware is the ability to become aware of problems. This unit is almost solely concerned with the forces that cause people to go from place to place, often unwillingly.

Closely linked with the ability to perceive problems is the skill to anticipate the events that result from the problems. In the case of "Comings and Goings," the student is to anticipate the consequences of such diverse happenings as a wedding and a war.

Preparing for the Unit

Unfortunately, human migrations are all too common these days. A tie-in with world events (or national events) will be relatively easy for you in administering this unit. "What would happen if" questions are sometimes very productive in terms of exciting the imaginations of young people and spurring them to think beyond given facts in a textbook. Although this unit utilizes that technique, it is far removed from the kind of question sometimes asked concerning the first voyage of Columbus (what if he had landed on the South American continent) or George Washington (what if he had accepted his followers' urgings to wear a crown). The speculation to be done in "Comings and Goings" ranges from the fanciful to the deadly serious.

Presenting the Unit and Following Through

The introductory sections of the unit are concerned with establishing the concept of migrating human beings. In all likelihood, your students are quite familiar with the idea of large groups of people migrating from one region to another. In a sense, the movement of people is what history chronicles. Nonetheless, anticipating what events will provoke the migrations of the next decade can be a fascinating mental exercise because our world is changing very rapidly. The so-called Third World is changing at a tremendous rate, and technological advances are changing the way much of the world lives. Could a bank robbery instigate a migration? Who knows!

"Comings and Goings" offers you an excellent chance to follow through with the musings, findings, hypothesizing, and so on, that should come out of this unit. The first activity that might come to your mind is to have your students describe the migration that they choose in the final section. The students are asked only to make a choice and then offer reasons for that choice. For those who are not overly fond of writing, other activities, such as drawing, dramatizing, debating, and reading, might be more appealing.

30 Comings and Goings

1 A migration is a pattern of behavior that certain highly mobile animals have adopted through an evolutionary process. Name at least three reasons for the migrations of animals.

2 We know that animals such as caribou, whales, wildebeest, and birds migrate every year, but what about humans? What kinds of people migrate to make sure they'll have enough food?

Are there people who migrate to a warmer climate each year? Who are they and where do they live?

Do you know of any other reasons for people to migrate? If so, what are they?

Facing the Issues © 1994 Zephyr Press, Tucson, Arizona

3 Which of the following events might result in a human migration? Circle the ones you think might cause a genuine migration of people.

a war	*a bank robbery*
a change of the heads of government	*a flood*
a soccer game	*the construction of a school*
a drought	*a technological invention*
a wedding	*the construction of a place of worship*

Of the ten events listed above, which is the most likely to result in the migration of people in the next decade? Tell why you think so.

31
Payback

Taking a Close Look at Retribution

Overview of the Unit

Although this unit is about retribution, not all of the examples of "paying back" are negative. Retribution is usually thought of in terms of vindictiveness, but there is a positive side to the concept also.

After they are given an introduction to the concept of retribution, your students are asked whether it is called for after five diverse incidents. Four of the incidents are of a kind that generally provokes retaliation; one is about a kindness at school.

Idea: Retribution Contributes to Human Misery and Ultimately Hurts Everyone Involved

"An eye for an eye and a tooth for a tooth" is advice that has been solemnly followed since before biblical times. Even today, many actions of individuals, communities, and nations are influenced, if not dictated, by the idea that retaliation is the only way to respond to an injustice or a crime. Human misery has multiplied as a result of this dictum. Feuds are, without exception, bad for everyone concerned.

Creative Thinking Skill to Be Developed: Being Sensitive and Aware

There are times when we take as a matter of course that there are injustices wreaked upon the innocent and that these oppressed people can do nothing to prevent their discomfiture. Generally, we believe those people can either turn the other cheek or they can seek revenge. What we want your students to recognize—to be sensitive to—is that there are several ways to look at, and to react to, negative and positive behaviors.

Preparing for the Unit

In all likelihood, you are aware that there are occasions when retaliation is about as frightening an idea as can be imagined, as, for example, when gangs strike back after an attack against one or more of their members. In certain communities, then, the idea of retribution is highly disturbing. We're purposely not offering gang warfare as an example of retribution. If the subject arises during the administering of "Payback," however, it might be a good idea to have a thorough discussion of that kind of retribution.

Presenting the Unit

This unit might not be as provocative as we envision it to be for your students, but it very well could induce as lively a discussion as you've had for some time. The anecdotes given may not have special significance for your students, and so we encourage you to substitute anecdotes that are more relevant in order that students become involved individually and collectively in investigating the concept, a most important one for nearly every kind of group and for individuals.

31 Payback

1 In basketball and football, there is such a thing as a "payback call." Players, coaches, and fans believe—but no referee admits—that when a decision (a "call") is made against a team unjustly, there will be another decision in its favor before long. People believe that some kind of justice is done in that way, but  they grumble about it. If the payback call is done to even things up, it is nonetheless a case of two wrongs trying to make a right, and that is not supposed to be good, or moral, in our society. A lot of harm has been done in the name of "righting a wrong." The term for this act is retribution.

Is there a time when retribution is truly justified? What about the following situations?

Someone steals a sandwich from your lunch, and you catch that person doing it. Is retribution called for? Explain.

An acquaintance notices that you are unable to open your locker because the combination lock just defeats you. The acquaintance hesitates while passing you and then offers to help. With the acquaintance's help, the lock finally opens. Is there any payback called for as a result of this kindness? Explain.

A bunch of students from a rival school burns an ugly emblem on the front lawn of your school. Should the students of your school do anything in return? Explain.

You are walking through the halls one day with two friends. One of them takes a big nail out of his pocket. As the three of you walk along, he gouges the wall on the right side of the hallway for about twenty feet. A teacher steps out in the hallway and sees your friend's senseless act. On the next day, you are called in to the assistant principal's office, and you are told that you will be suspended for three days and you must pay for repainting the wall. You are dumbfounded because you didn't gouge the wall—your friend did. It so happened that you were the only one of the trio whom the teacher recognized. You aren't going to name your friend, but you vehemently protest your innocence. The assistant principal clearly doesn't believe you and isn't interested in your protestations. Does retribution play any role here? If so, who gets paid back—the assistant principal, your friend, or the teacher who turned you in? Explain.

2 An airplane is skyjacked by terrorists from a country known to support such violations of international law. The airplane is diverted to an airport in a country that is very tough concerning such acts. When it lands, the airplane is surrounded by armed police, and the terrorists are ordered to release all of the passengers and crew and give themselves up. Instead, they murder everyone in the airplane and try to escape. They are all captured except one, who is killed when fleeing. The passengers and crew are mostly from a third country, which was the flight's original destination.

Is retribution called for by the country who has lost its citizens? Since this kind of terrorism is a serious worldwide problem, a satisfactory solution must be reached. What do you suggest? Give reasons for the steps or measures that must be taken.

Payback *(continued)*

148

Facing the Issues © 1994 Zephyr Press, Tucson, Arizona

32
Riddles for Our Times

Thinking about the Community

Overview of the Unit

This unit consists only of a set of seven riddles and a question about which of the seven answers to the riddles affects the students' community most. The riddles all have to do with community living. We expect that they will be challenging to most of your students, but they should not be too difficult to solve if enough time is allotted for completing the unit.

You might want to ask yourself the seven questions before administering the unit. Besides alerting yourself to the nuances, pitfalls, dead ends, ramifications, and so on, that may be encountered, you can judge how well the questions might be handled by your students.

Idea: There Are Forces in a Community that Affect Everyone in It

This unit is designed to make your students more aware of what is going on in their community.

Creative Thinking Skill to Be Developed: Putting Ideas into Context

The essential skill involved in this riddling activity is one of matching. In looking for answers to riddles, we try to find something that meets certain requirements, the stipulated characteristics or conditions set forth in the question. This fitting together is a basic form of putting ideas into context. Riddles provide a way of communicating an idea in a highly effective way because they deal with everyday matters. The folk wisdom that can be found in a riddle is often achieved by showing something in a different (and often humorous) light.

Preparing for the Unit

Since there isn't much warm-up written into "Riddles for Our Times," it would be advisable for you to engage your students in a discussion of riddles before administering the unit. Younger children love riddles, and maybe some of that fondness has been retained by your students. This unit has the advantage of consisting mostly of a gamelike activity. Many scholars have noted that playfulness is a marked characteristic of creative people engaged in producing novel ideas. Although to some educators it seems out of place in the classroom, playfulness, when engaged in purposefully, frees up creative energies in ways nothing else can.

Presenting the Unit

For this unit, we recommend you put your students on their own or in pairs. Depending upon their abilities and backgrounds, "Riddles for Our Times" could be a difficult assignment. Our intent is not to frustrate or stymie your students, but to stretch their minds. If the activity does look to be fairly difficult, having your students working in pairs is probably a good idea.

Only to satisfy your curiosity about how our minds work, here are some possible answers to the riddles. We want to emphasize that these aren't the "correct" answers. Your students may come up with answers that are better. You may have other, better ideas too.

What gives but never takes? A clock in a public place, such as city hall

What takes but seldom gives? The garbage collector

What usually slows down when it is hurried? Various kinds of municipal service (bureaucratic red tape)

What comes quickly, disappears, and comes quickly again? Public outrage

What returns when it isn't watched? An epidemic such as tuberculosis or influenza

What is powerful but not dangerous? Public goodwill

What is safer when it is isolated? A false rumor; a homicidal maniac

32 Riddles for Our Times

Here are some items that are basic to living in any community. All of them affect the quality of life of the people in your community. See if you can identify them.

What gives but never takes?

What takes but seldom gives?

What usually slows down when it is hurried?

What comes quickly, disappears, and comes quickly again?

What returns when it isn't watched?

What is powerful but not dangerous?

What is safer when it is isolated?

Which of those things you have named affects your community most?

Why does it affect your community?

══════ 33 ══════
A Marshmallow Summer

Suggesting Improvements in Communicating

Overview of the Unit

There are a lot of questions in this unit. Some are nonsensical, and some are very serious. The five contrived ones are generally enigmatic and off-beat. Deliberately so. We want to stretch the minds of your students a little. All of the questions, from "Do marshmallows come in the summer?" to "Is autumn after crickets?" are answerable. Your students are capable of explaining each of them, but some may not want to. These questions aren't the kinds all young people enjoy. Some of your students won't readily "play the game" and invent little rationalizations or stories to make the questions sensible. Because our purpose is to get students to think about communications problems in society, you shouldn't be disturbed by their rejecting the activity. Just steer them down to the last level, where they are asked for suggestions about solving society's communication problems.

Idea: By Improving Their Communications Skills, People Can Improve Their Lives

Underlying the ambiguities in this unit is the idea that we can live better and fuller lives by learning to communicate more accurately and affectively.

Creative Thinking Skills to Be Developed: Looking from a Different Perspective

This unit combines critical thinking and creative thinking, but not simultaneously. The zany questions in the middle of the unit are meant to be mind-stretchers, but the final question about improving communications in society involves your students in evaluating and analyzing, although your students may well offer ingenious solutions to society's communications problems. As a matter of fact, we desperately need some originality of thinking in order to solve our more serious problems in communicating on many levels.

Preparing for the Unit

"A Marshmallow Summer" is not an ordinary sort of exercise. Its questions are not the kind that teachers are accustomed to asking or pupils to answering. For just this reason, the questions may annoy and frustrate some students while they challenge and delight others. If both teachers and students receive the questions in an open-minded manner, the questions can lead to considerable excitement. If, on the other hand, they are presented and received without a spirit of inquiry, the questions will be of little value.

Because the exercise is unusual, you should prepare your students for it with some kind of warm-up. You might ask them how they feel about people who ask questions that have obvious answers. (Some people ask only rhetorical questions, it seems.) You might also lead in to the unit with a riddle. A riddle that has some humor would be a good choice. After some preliminary stage-setting, then, you can present the unit with more assurance that your students will be receptive to the oddball questions.

Presenting the Unit

After some general questions about questions, the unit poses these five questions:

Do marshmallows come in the summer?

Where is yesterday?

Does your radio always glare like that?

What comes after "z"?

Is autumn after crickets?

Each of the questions can be dealt with symbolically or literally, logically or illogically, seriously or flippantly, peevishly or good-humoredly, superficially or philosophically. Although this type of unit has been administered, with some success, as both an oral exercise and a written exercise, we recommend that your students answer the questions individually at first in order to avoid possible outbreaks of smart-aleckness. Depending upon students' reactions, you can have a general discussion of their responses before they tackle the last part of the unit. Since the last section is entirely serious, it may be best to have your students go it alone through the end of the unit.

To give you an idea of how someone might respond to the first question about marshmallows in the summer, here are some reactions of our students:

Yes, along with sticks and a fire on the beach.

Marshmallows and summer aren't necessarily related. I like marshmallows in my chocolate in the winter.

Only in my dreams, when there are also grazing cows and periwinkles.

Right after the trolls and leprechauns.

Yes, and in the spring, fall, and winter too.

The five questions are like many things in life: what at first seems impossible or ridiculous turns out to be quite plausible.

33 A Marshmallow Summer

1 How do you feel about people asking silly questions? Have you ever laughed at a question that you thought was silly or absurd and found out that the person asking the question was quite serious? If so, what was the situation?

How do you feel about questions that have more than one right answer? Does it bother you that there isn't just one right answer?

2 Here are some questions that may seem crazy to you, but maybe you can make sense out of them. Try to answer each of the questions, regardless of how silly it seems.

Do marshmallows come in the summer? Why do you think so?

Where is yesterday? Explain.

Does your radio always glare like that? Why or why not?

A Marshmallow Summer (continued)

What comes after "z"? Explain your answer.

Is autumn after crickets? Why or why not?

3 When someone says something you don't understand, what can you do to understand him or her better?

4 In what ways can we improve communications so that people can live better and fuller lives?

═══34═══
Avalanches

Using "Avalanche" as a Metaphor

Overview of the Unit

This unit deals with the avalanche concept. After a discussion of landslides and avalanches, there is a section in which your students are asked to supply seven sentences in which the word *avalanche* is used metaphorically. Finally, students are to designate one of those avalanches as the one that concerns them most. Since the seven items vary from personal to public interest, the discussion could be wide-ranging.

Idea: The Idea of "Avalanche" Is Deeply Imbedded in the Human Psyche and Is a Metaphor for Many Important Events

In playing with the word in this unit, your students will have an opportunity also to obtain insights about political processes.

Creative Thinking Skill to Be Developed: Putting Ideas into Context

We probably don't think we are using the skill of putting ideas into context when we employ a metaphor in our speaking or writing, but in a rudimentary way we are. We consciously or unconsciously choose a certain metaphor and apply it to a particular situation. In the case of a metaphor such as "we blew them away," which has been a cliché in recent years, someone uses the expression for an occasion in which a group of people has been overwhelmed or dispensed with quickly. "Avalanche" hasn't attained the status of a cliché, but its use is common enough so that we readily understand a sentence such as: "An avalanche of dissent meant a resounding defeat for the measure."

Preparing for the Unit

There will probably be many times when a student makes use of a common metaphor in a class discussion. Such an occasion can be used to lead into this unit, or you can find one or more examples in the daily newspaper. The unit will work best if you do introduce it with a few appropriate words—perhaps something relating to the everyday lives of your students. On the other hand, there is enough of a warm-up at the beginning of the unit for you to administer it "cold," that is, without a lead-in or build-up.

Presenting the Unit

Our ulterior motive is to get your students to discuss regional or national issues. Therefore, the final question is the important element in this unit. After allowing students enough time to think fairly deeply about which avalanche really concerns them, you should allow your students to discuss their ideas in a completely open discussion.

34 Avalanches

1 Have you ever seen a landslide? If so, where was it?

Have you ever seen an avalanche? If so, where did you see one?

What is the difference between a landslide and an avalanche?

Where did the word *avalanche* come from?

During presidential elections we hear and read about landslides, but a "landslide victory" for a candidate may mean that the candidate receives only 55 percent of the popular vote. The "landslide" is seen in the count of the electoral votes.

We are more likely to use avalanche than landslide, however, in ordinary discourse. We can use the word in a number of ways. You might say, "An avalanche of negative public opinion was critical in the decision of Senator Holsum to oppose the measure."

2 How could you use avalanche in commenting about the following phenomena:

Junk mail

Personal bills (money owed creditors)

Assignments and tasks at school

Opinions about timber harvesting in the Northwest

Bills before Congress

Letters of protest to congressional leaders concerning Medicare reform

Complaints about abuse of power by elected officials

3 Which of these avalanches concerns you most? Why?

35

How Worthy?

Considering the Idea of Creditworthiness

Overview of the Unit

The subject of this unit, credit, is an important one for young people to grasp. Ultimately, the concepts of credit and confidence are bound together in today's economic fabric. Like trust, credit is an important asset for any individual to have.

Opening with a discussion of the notion of commercial credit, the unit then asks your students to consider the role that credit plays in the lives of individuals, businesses, and nations. Finally, they are asked about the essential nature of credit.

Although familiarity with business practices will help your students in this unit, it isn't necessary when they start to conceive of the ramifications of having or not having creditworthiness. As you know, the consequences are serious for most people. Moreover, more young people are being offered credit cards in colleges and universities these days, and the easy accessibility of that kind of personal credit should be considered by your students prior to their being in a position to respond to the offers.

Idea: Credit Can Be Equated with Confidence or Trust and Is Precious

Whether one considers it in terms of finances or integrity, creditworthiness is an extremely valuable asset.

Creative Thinking Skill to Be Developed: Imagining Consequences

When engaged in thinking about the role of credit for various people, businesses, and governments, your students are put into the position of imagining the consequences of having or not having credit. According to the small-business person as well as to the chief executive officer of a large corporation, credit is all-important to the success of the enterprise. (Oddly enough, the larger the business, the more it depends upon some-one else's money.) To be able to respond to the ten items, your students will have to imagine situations in which credit is given or denied. This kind of thinking is akin to hypothesis making, a very important skill in creative and scientific endeavors.

Preparing for and Presenting the Unit

A good time to look into the subject of credit is any time your students are studying or discussing some aspect of business—either local, national, or international. The International Monetary Fund, World Bank, and im-portant treaties can't be fully understood unless the concept of credit is grasped. However, our purpose is to coax your students into thinking about their own relationships with financial credit. For a majority of them, credit will become terribly important before long. They will have encounters with credit at crucial points in their lives: when entering a post-secondary school, setting up housekeeping, having children, start-ing a business, being admitted to a hospital, and so on. If credit is in-volved in personal worth, then it is a very important concept to consider.

Because there is a good deal offered in this unit insofar as its scope is concerned, you may want to allow your students more than one class period to respond to the ideas presented in it. In fact, the introduction and the activity about the creditworthiness of the various individuals, firms, and governments should probably be administered individually, followed by a group discussion, and the last section dealt with in a suc-ceeding session. Your students may have already had experiences with credit in one form or another, and so the final discussion could be most interesting.

35 How Worthy?

1 Is it good to be a creditor? Usually it is, but not always. When would it be better to be a debtor than to be a creditor?

The United States is now a "debtor nation," whereas until recently it was a "creditor nation." Put simply, that just means we owe more to other countries than they owe to us. It seems that the old-fashioned notion of "neither a lender nor a borrower be" isn't relevant these days, and it hasn't been since the advent of the credit card. Our economy is based upon the idea that we can buy today and pay tomorrow. Bankruptcies are epidemic in the country, both for corporations and individuals. It's easy to "charge it."

2 It is not uncommon for people who have "good credit" to be solicited three or four times in a month by banks offering credit cards. Those people are considered "creditworthy." Creditworthiness has become a rather important idea in recent times. When a person, business, institution, or nation is rated creditworthy, things can happen that otherwise can't happen.

What difference would it make to the following individuals, businesses, and governments if they were or were not considered creditworthy?

A professional football team

A shoe repairman in a large city

How Worthy? *(continued)*

A producer of concerts

A consultant to cities regarding urban development

A private college

El Salvador

An owner of a racetrack

A protestant minister in a small town

A gasoline service station

A metropolitan city in the United States

3 Is credit a matter of *confidence* in the character of someone or something? Does it show that the world believes in you if you are creditworthy, as one television commercial has suggested? Why or why not?

What is credit, anyway?

Facing the Issues © 1994 Zephyr Press, Tucson, Arizona

36

The Institution
as an Organism

Comparing Human Beings and Institutions

Overview of the Unit

An analogy between the growth of human beings and the growth of institutions is made in this unit. The unit is based upon that extended metaphor and nothing else. Accordingly, the unit is mostly an intellectual exercise for your students; except for their gaining insights about social institutions, they probably won't be able to make any immediate practical application of what they receive from encountering this unit.

Following two paragraphs about the relationship of nurturance and development in humans, we present the idea that the social institutions may benefit and suffer from similar conditions in their histories. (Note that we don't define a social institution. We leave that up to the students.) Your students are then asked to select an institution that has exhibited humanlike tendencies in its development.

Idea: Social Institutions Behave in Many Ways as Do Living Organisms

The analogy of living (and dying) organisms can be applied with profit to an analysis of social institutions.

Creative Thinking Skill to Be Developed: Putting Ideas into Context

Usually it is fun for students to play with analogies, and frequently they can learn from doing so. We're hoping that our inviting your students to think of a social institution as a human being will be somewhat amusing for them. They should be able to make a few connections and see similarities between the growth of a child and a newly formed institution. Analogizing has proved to be an effective way to see hitherto unrevealed aspects of all kinds of animate and inanimate things. Several creative problem-solving procedures depend heavily upon analogizing to help individuals and groups find novel solutions to problems.

Preparing for the Unit

"The Institution as an Organism" is not a long or complicated unit. We simply present the idea, albeit a somewhat sophisticated one, that a social institution can be likened to a human being when it comes to the importance of nurturance. To warm up your students, you might use a simile, analogy, or some other form of metaphor. For example, you could note that shopping malls are still sprouting up around the country like dandelions (or you could find a more flattering comparison). Then you could inquire as to whether that simile could stand some analysis. Such an interchange might well set the stage for our statement about a social institution's needing nurturance in its formative stages.

Presenting the Unit

Except for the last section, this unit might be given orally; that is, a discussion can effectively follow the points made in the first section. However, your students should respond individually to the challenge to name an institution that exhibits recuperative powers but also needs love and attention. In that way, the stronger personalities and the scholastic "stars" won't exert undue influence upon students who are either impressionable or unsure of their own abilities to produce imaginative ideas.

36   The Institution as an Organism

Getting enough food to stay alive is a problem for too many children today. If, however, children who have been starving then get enough food continuously thereafter, they achieve normal growth and function as healthy adults. Human beings have amazing recuperative powers, even when they are malnourished for extended periods of time.

If a child is deprived of love and attention, especially in the first year, he or she will not grow at a normal rate. This relationship between nurturance and physical growth has been found in all human societies. In addition, most often the child will be permanently impaired emotionally.

Could these two principles be seen in areas other than the growth of human beings? For example, could social institutions be seen as recovering from malnourishment and then developing normally? And could they suffer from neglect and then never function normally for the rest of their history? Which institution in our society that particularly exhibits tendencies in its development can be explained by these two principles? Give a rationale for your choice, and then provide some examples of how the institution has "behaved" in cases of deprivation.

$$===37===$$

Looking a Gift Horse
in the Mouth

Examining the Consequences of Giving Gifts

Overview of the Unit

This unit is an example of reversing something in order to take another look at it. In this case, we are asking your students to look at good deeds that can backfire on the donor. We ask them to imagine how giving seven items might have unfortunate consequences. Your students are then asked to give an example of a situation in which withholding and not offering something might produce good results. Finally, they are asked to give an example of when it would be better for the receiver to decline the gift.

Idea: Giving Can Be Either Selfish or Unselfish

In some cultures gift giving is a terribly important element in the social fabric, holding things together. In the United States it is sometimes regarded as an act that puts the receiver in the position of being obligated to the giver.

Creative Thinking Skill to Be Developed: Looking from a Different Perspective

"Looking a Gift Horse in the Mouth" has your students turning things around. One can always look at any event from a point of view different from the obvious one. For example, when it comes to gift giving, some people look for an ulterior motive, that is, what's the giver trying to get? The approach in this unit is more about unexpected consequences. If you've ever given somebody something you expected would be warmly received and have been terribly disappointed, you know that, in retrospect, looking at the event from another perspective (that of the person receiving the gift) might have allowed you to avoid the unpleasant experience.

Preparing for the Unit

Setting the stage for this unit should require only a few words regarding surprises. We know that some adults don't like surprises, but it seems as if young people associate surprises with pleasant experiences. You might explore this difference with your students before administering the unit.

Presenting the Unit

The format of this unit is typical of all units in *Facing the Issues.* That is, there is an introduction, and then an activity is proposed in which students are supposed to respond to a series of items. Then they are given a task (in this unit, imagining a situation in which someone should refuse a gift). Generally speaking, you can accompany your students while they proceed through the first portion of the unit, and then you should let them finish up individually. The first section or two, then, is a warm-up for the last part of the unit. We value independent thinking, and we therefore hope that the individual student will be encouraged to come up with ideas of his or her own in the culminating phase of the unit.

37 Looking a Gift Horse in the Mouth

1 The world is full of good-hearted, generous people. Most of us are pleased to give a helping hand to those in need, and almost everyone knows the satisfaction of having provided comfort, money, clothing, or food for another human being. On the other hand, the best-intentioned actions sometimes produce mischief, woe, and even tragedy. There are times when a gift such as a car, motorcycle, video game, or large sum of money has extremely unfortunate consequences.

How can each of the following intended good deeds backfire for the person who wants to help another?

Giving an animal as a gift to someone

Bequeathing a building to be shared equally by heirs

Helping someone do his or her homework

Giving a trip as a present

Looking a Gift Horse in the Mouth (continued)

Introducing to each other two people of whom you are very fond

Offering to help people resolve their differences

2 Give an example of a situation where holding back and not offering something can have good results.

Facing the Issues © 1994 Zephyr Press, Tucson, Arizona

173

3 Give an example of a situation in which the person on the receiving end is better served by refusing.

38

Come Again?

Interpreting Ambiguous Statements

Overview of the Unit

"Come Again" is short by the standards of most units in this book. It has, nevertheless, the potential to be a challenging unit. After an introduction concerning paradoxical statements, your students are asked to interpret seven statements. Each of the statements can be accepted as being true if interpreted in a certain way, and in so doing we hope your students throw a little light upon their world.

Idea: Ambiguous Statements Often Contain a Kernel of Truth or Wisdom

The problem with ambiguous statements is that they cause us to think!

Creative Thinking Skill to Be Developed: Looking from a Different Perspective

In "Come Again?" we ask your students to interpret seven somewhat discordant statements. All of the statements make good sense if seen in the proper light. None is supposed to be striking in its wisdom; they qualify more as paradoxical statements than as aphorisms. But because of the nature of the statements, your students will have to <u>think</u> in order to "detect the truth or wisdom in each."

Preparing for the Unit

Choosing the right time for some lessons is often the key decision. This unit is the kind that should be administered when your students are in the proper mood. That mood can be described as being thoughtful, somewhat serious, and inquisitive. Your students might also be a little cocksure. If the timing is right, the unit will produce considerable thinking and perhaps some investigation.

Presenting the Unit

This unit will be most effective if a discussion follows the individual efforts of your students to make sense of the seven statements. The statements are ambiguous, but, more important, they are provocative. Therefore, your students should attempt to struggle with them before a general discussion yields various interpretations and refutations.

We are very reluctant to offer our interpretations of the statements because we really have few predilections when it comes to giving genuine meaning to them. Nevertheless, here are some slantings concerning each of the statements.

One of the best ways to get an honest opinion is to consult a fool. There is a conviction on the part of many people that fools will give direct answers when knowledgeable people equivocate.

The easiest thing I've ever done was the most challenging. When you start out to perform a task, it often turns out to be far more difficult than you thought at the outset.

It's the thinking that gets you in trouble. When performing certain physical tasks, as in athletic competition, it doesn't pay to think too much about all of the aspects, mechanics, or possibilities of the act to be performed.

Superstition is the salvation of humanity. Some have equated superstition with a belief in the supernatural, which has saved many an individual's peace of mind.

Capitalism is closer to warfare than is matrimony. Capitalism presumes everyone is out to get the most for his or her services, whereas matrimony presumes some (or a lot) of cooperation and some (or a lot) of self-sacrifice.

Painting is a subtle form of masochism. Getting a painting "just right" is a tricky, tedious, demanding, and frustrating business.

No definition of democracy should include a reference to freedom. Democracy's main feature is government by the will of the many; the emphasis is NOT upon the individual's freedom but upon his or her responsibilities.

You may well disagree with any or all of the positions taken above. We intend merely to give possible interpretations of the statements. Similarly, we would expect your students to disagree with one another about the statements. Some additional learning should result if the anticipated debates take place.

38   Come Again?

"Sometimes you can see more by using your ears." A statement such as this can make you wonder if someone hasn't gotten his or her words tangled up, but there is a good deal to it. As old-timers can tell you, radio dramas produced a multitude of vivid pictures in the minds of listeners, whereas television dramas tend to do all the seeing for us.

Occasionally we read or hear an expression that makes us ponder, or it may even confuse us. Upon reflection, we can see an element of truth—or even wisdom—in the statement. Here are seven such statements, all of which have a kernel of truth. See if you can detect the truth or wisdom in each. Tell how each statement can give us an insight about living in today's world.

One of the best ways to get an honest opinion is to consult a fool.

The easiest thing I've ever done was the most challenging.

It's the thinking that gets you in trouble.

Superstition is the salvation of humanity.

Capitalism is closer to warfare than is matrimony.

Facing the Issues © 1994 Zephyr Press, Tucson, Arizona

Painting is a subtle form of masochism.

No definition of democracy should include a reference to freedom.

═══39═══
Changing the World

Imagining Transformations to Improve the World

Overview of the Unit

In some important respects, "Changing the World" is the most challenging of the units in this book. Nearly all of the ten items your students are asked to transform will cause them to think deeply. Perhaps the easiest is the first: "What would be more beautiful if it were more accessible?" Like the others, it can be responded to in a number of ways, but we hope that it isn't responded to superficially.

This is one of only a few units that simply offers an introduction and a series of items to be responded to. The final item, "What one thing do you want to change most?" is probably the important part. We suggest that you have your students respond to it privately at first.

Idea: The Only Constant Is Change

Many people, as they grow old, try to resist change. It's impossible, of course. Fortunately for the young, they accept change as being natural, which it is.

Creative Thinking Skill to Be Developed:
Being Sensitive and Aware; Seeing Relationships

A major component of the skill, being sensitive and aware, is being sensitive to problems. "Changing the World" is designed to alert your students to problems of which they are aware but need to think about more.

This unit combines critical thinking (analyzing, comparing, and judging) with creative thinking (being sensitive and aware, seeing relationships) in such a way that the two kinds of thinking are completely integrated.

Preparing for and Presenting the Unit

The success of "Changing the World" as a learning experience may depend upon how it is introduced to a class. This type of exercise has been fairly effective when administered without a warm-up by the teacher, but it is most successful when the stage has been set for its appearance and when the students see some reason for searching their minds for ways to improve things.

Motivation for this unit will depend upon the makeup of your class and their previous experiences with activities of this type. Nevertheless, you can do a great deal to help your students to use their imagination by removing as many inhibiting factors from the situation as possible. Eliminate any threat of evaluation; grades appear to be incompatible with exercises that seek to promote creative thinking. Allow your students as much time as possible to finish the unit. It will take the thoughtful ones longer than those who are usually in a hurry to finish any task. Tell your students not to be too concerned with their neighbors' ideas. This unit should be done solo. There is too much risk of some students becoming silly or snide when they encounter the items dealing with kindness, intelligence, happiness, and the like for a general discussion to go as well as individual responses.

"Changing the World" does entail some risk for you. The risk may be minimal if you have the kind of students with which we have sometimes been blessed to be associated. Knowing how your students will respond, however, is itself a problematical business. Sometimes you can be thrilled with their perspicacity and insightfulness.

39 Changing the World

Changes are taking place all the time, but some of the changes make our lives worse instead of better. Because of the continuing increases in population all over the world and especially in the so-called underdeveloped countries, we are experiencing problems in areas such as the pollution of the skies and seas that were not even topics of conversation fifty years ago. On the other hand, you may have felt grateful at times for changes you think will come in the next several years. Following are ten changes that might improve the world. Give your choices for the improvements and tell why.

What would be more beautiful if it were more accessible?

What should be smaller so that it would be more economical?

What would be kinder if it were smarter?

What would be more efficient if it were underground?

What would be more colorful if it were regimented?

What would be more just if it were more intelligent?

Changing the World *(continued)*

What would be healthier if it were more law-abiding?

What should be bigger so that it could be more democratic?

What would be more valuable if it were flatter?

What would be happier if it were free?

What one thing do you want to change most? Why?

===40===
Celebrate!

Scrutinizing Our National Holidays

Overview of the Unit

"Celebrate!" is offbeat as a social studies lesson, but it can still be a springboard for learning. Your students may be aware that in this country practically every day of the year is officially dedicated to something, many of which are commercial products and services. We have a day for secretaries, bosses, dairy products, books, beef, healthy hearts, groundhogs, grandparents, and so on. None of those days is a national holiday, however, and so they can be ignored by the majority of the populace. It would be fascinating for one or more of your students to determine the names of all the days dedicated to people, products, services, and institutions during the year.

In this unit, we propose sixteen unlikely reasons for a national "fun" holiday. We stipulate that these holidays wouldn't be so serious as to call for no work (nowadays that usually happens on Monday, anyway), but they would be in the spirit of casual celebrating, with decorations, outings, and greetings. We ask your students how each of these spurious holidays could be celebrated. Finally, we ask which groups benefit most from national holidays.

Idea: We Might Have One More National Holiday, and It Could Be as Frivolous as Some of the Others Are Inane

Although there is a whimsical, if not cynical, tone to this unit, you could really challenge the reason for our having so many holidays when you present this unit to your students.

Creative Thinking Skills to Be Developed: Being Original; Seeing Relationships; Anticipating Consequences

By proposing the "unusual" national holidays, we intend to provoke your students into using their imaginations. For example, to come up with ways of celebrating a holiday such as "National Dandelion Day," they must imagine a world in which dandelions are honored (or scorned). If honored, the dandelions can be used as articles of adornment (garlands, decorations for the hair, bracelets, boutonnieres) or food and drink (vegetables for salads and wine). A student might also think of a day in which people attempt to remove dandelions from lawns, gardens, and fields. (Fat chance!)

The final question is designed to cause your students to see the tie-ins of holidays with such groups as the travel industry, restaurants, the entertainment industry (including theaters and amusement parks), and the automotive and petroleum industries. There was obviously some connection between the economic health of those groups and the government's switching the celebration of the holidays (except for two or three) to Mondays.

Preparing for the Unit

The obvious time to administer this unit is before or after a holiday. For a great majority of your students, holidays are eagerly anticipated and highly valued. Consequently, there should be sufficient interest in thinking about them to motivate some intriguing responses after contemplating our phony holidays.

Presenting the Unit

Whether you take your students through this unit orally or not will probably depend upon their age and sophistication. We can imagine that it would be more effective if a discussion were to take place after your students have completed the section about ways of celebrating the sixteen holidays and then another one when all of your students have completed the entire unit.

The section dealing with the consequences of actually having three of those holidays probably should be done individually. It may well be the most interesting part of the unit for both you and your students.

40 Celebrate!

We have some sacred holidays, and we have some fun holidays such as Valentine's Day and Halloween. Neither of those days, however, is a national holiday, when banks close and mail isn't delivered. Perhaps we need some more fun holidays. Businesses wouldn't close, as most do for Thanksgiving, but we could do as some people do in foreign countries and hike up a mountain or hang up some decorations and exchange greetings.

We could celebrate any number of things. Here are a few that we might celebrate. Describe what all of us might do to celebrate the following things:

Clean laundry

Left-handers

Hamburgers

Television commercials (or no television commercials)

Facing the Issues © 1994 Zephyr Press, Tucson, Arizona

People with green eyes

Letter writing

Jeans

Space exploration

Courtesy

Chicken

Dandelions

Celebrate! *(continued)*

Agriculture

Honesty

"Monopoly"

Pets

T-shirts

Celebrate! *(continued)*

Take three of your proposed holidays and tell what might happen if they actually were adopted.

Which groups of people benefit most from national holidays? Why do you think so?

=41=
Nature Versus Humans

Contemplating the Forces of Nature and Using Natural Resources

Overview of the Unit

First, this unit addresses the consequences of natural phenomena such as earthquakes, hurricanes, floods, landslides, and avalanches. We know there is nothing (as yet) that we can do to prevent natural disasters. We can only prepare for them. Even preparing and taking precautions will not always prevent tremendous damage and suffering.

On the other hand, people can relocate soil and water, and we can harness the wind. In this unit, your students are asked to think of the positive effects that result when we perform those kinds of operations.

Idea: Relocating Natural Elements such as Earth and Water Can Produce Important Benefits

Homo sapiens has evolved into a creature who aspires to change the face of Earth. In a very true sense, we have taken possession of the planet.

Creative Thinking Skills to Be Developed: Producing Alternatives; Combining Ideas and Elements

Your students are asked to name at least five good results that can happen as a result of utilizing earth, water, and wind. By listing the results, they will be practicing a fundamental creative thinking skill, namely, producing alternatives. Inasmuch as there is no time restriction for this unit (that is, there should not be any), the student shouldn't feel that she or he is under any pressure to produce the fifteen results quickly. If any student wants to go beyond the requested fifteen responses for using soil, water, and air, she or he should be encouraged to do so.

Generally speaking, the more ideas produced the greater likelihood of one or more ideas being original or useful. In the case of "Nature Versus Humans" we aren't looking for unusual responses until your students reach the last section. In that part, they are asked to think of what good things can happen when the three elements are combined in pairs.

Preparing for the Unit

Although this unit can be administered in conjunction with any number of curricular topics and activities, it probably would be of particular interest after the occurrence of a natural disaster. The emphasis of the unit, however, is not upon the awful consequences of a natural disaster, but the imaginations of young people are necessarily engaged when reflecting upon the awesome powers of nature after an earthquake or hurricane.

The concerns expressed daily for the soils, forests, oceans, lakes, rivers, and atmosphere are also appropriate topics for leading into this unit.

Presenting the Unit

If your purpose in administering this unit is to have your students reflect about how humans struggle with the forces of nature in order to provide themselves with food, shelter, comfort, transportation, recreation, and so on, then it may work best as an individual effort by your students, followed by a general discussion when they have finished with it. When your students respond individually, the range of ideas for the section in which they list good results will probably be quite broad, and their responses could even be more diverse when they combine elements of air, water, and earth in the last section.

41 Nature Versus Humans

If we look at a standing body of water such as a lake, it can be beautiful, and as such it is an aesthetic delight. The body of water can also be a wonderful resource for boaters, swimmers, and fishermen. If that body of water is caused to move, however, any number of practical purposes can be achieved, from generating electricity to milling wheat.

If we look at a field of snow, it also can be very pleasing to the eye and a delight to cross-country skiers and snowmobilers. Snow set in motion on the side of a mountain, however, can knock down trees, hurl boulders downward, and engulf people and animals.

When we look at a hill, it too is often a pleasant sight. If the soil of the hill is made to move, however, it, like the snow, can cause serious damage. Houses, sheds, cars, gardens, and so on, can be inundated in a mudslide.

It is apparent, then, that natural phenomena such as water, air, snow, and soil can serve people very well or they can cause great damage. When they are out of control and move in great quantities, as is the case with floods, volcanic eruptions, earthquakes, hurricanes, and landslides, tragedy can result. Whereas too much water, soil, and air can cause great harm, the right amount of water, soil, and air can do much good. People take it upon themselves to relocate those resources for their own purposes.

Name at least five good results that can happen as a consequence of moving a bucketful of water.

Name at least five good results that can happen as a consequences of moving a shovelful of soil.

Name at least five good events that can transpire as a result of a gust of wind.

Can you think of three good results from combining two of those elements? What good things can happen if you combine the movement of water with the movement of air or soil, or if you combine the movement of soil and air? Choose one of the three combinations.

42

A Hole in One

Examining the Idea That Less Can Be Better

Overview of the Unit

The unit begins with a narrative about a high school teacher who offers to his class the idea that sometimes "less is better." Obviously it is if you are overweight, as he points out. We also ask your students to consider whether less is better in the area of self-improvement and in the fields of transportation, communications, and government. "A Hole in One" ends with your students being asked if they can apply the same principle to their own lives in order to make themselves more productive.

Idea: Sometimes Less Is More.

This unit is related to unit 9, "Is Bigger Better?" You might note the differences in the reactions to one of the units after presenting the other.

Creative Thinking Skill to Be Developed: Producing Alternatives

You may think that there is a bit too much demand placed upon your students to come up with ideas in this unit. They are asked to produce alternatives in five categories. In our experience (and in the experience of people who help others think more creatively), the better ideas come after the first, obvious responses are given. (Perhaps we should have asked for a dozen responses in each category.) The great majority of individuals don't produce their most inspired ideas at the beginning of their efforts to think of many alternatives. After they have got out a number of obvious, mundane, and predictable ideas, their minds begin to see hidden meanings and find unexpected relationships. They begin to produce "wild" ideas, some of which, when evaluated after the ideation session is over, may turn out to be excellent.

Preparing for and Presenting the Unit

Probably the best way to administer this unit is to follow the lead of Hal Roberts. Bring a frisbee to class and ask your students how it is that a frisbee can fly so far. Then show them an "aerobie." Quiz them concerning the aerodynamics of the two discs in an effort to find out how the one with the hole in the middle flies farther. Then have them work in pairs for twenty minutes to produce a list of objects that perform in a "superior" manner when a part of them is removed. After discussing their suggestions, put the two lists of objects on the chalkboard, with one column containing the original objects and the other naming the "superior" model.

After the class has discussed each of the objects on the board and its inherent merits, devote a few minutes to comparing the concept of reduction in human beings. When is less actually more? (You can cite the size of an individual in a very cramped space.) Then you can compare the physical aspects of reduction with that found in behavior (for example, watching less television provides more time for homework or active pursuits). You can then easily direct this line of thinking into the area of positive human relationships, when withholding emotions and eliminating offensive behaviors can lead to improved relationships. Of course, the idea of less-can-be-more can be applied to positive relationships between entire societies, as for example in the elimination of nuclear weapons.

A little bit, or all, of the above can be carried out as a warm-up for the unit. As we have hinted, there is no end to what might be done with this concept.

42   A Hole in One

One day Hal Roberts, a high school teacher, brought a frisbee to class. He held it up and asked, "How is it that a frisbee can fly so far?" The class offered a number of ideas. Then Mr. Roberts showed them an "aerobie," a toy similar to the frisbee but with most of its center missing. He explained that the aerobie can fly even farther than the frisbee. Mr. Roberts then remarked that sometimes less is better and gave the class the examples of short hair's being more easily managed than long hair and that eating less can be better for your health. Do you agree with his argument? Why or why not?

Perhaps the idea that reducing something can result in an improvement is worth looking into. Can you think of three examples in the area of self-improvement?

What can you think of in the field of transportation that can be improved by reducing it? Name at least three things.

What about the field of communications—can you think of three things that can be improved by reducing them?

What about government? Many, many people have called for reducing government. What three things would you reduce in government?

What three things can be reduced in your own life that will make you more productive?

43

These Oxys
Aren't for Morons

Composing Oxymorons for Individuals, Institutions, and Organizations

Overview of the Unit

These days the word oxymoron is almost a cliché. Several years back we didn't have so many book titles, movie titles, and the like employing the device, but nowadays expressions such as "back to the future" are commonplace. Nevertheless, this unit deals only with that figure of speech, and we still have some hope that, although not as special as it once was, the oxymoron will appeal to your students.

After a brief introduction, the unit leads your students into an activity in which they are to interpret seven oxymorons. Having offered explanations of the oxymorons, your students are then asked to invent oxymorons to fit eight individuals, institutions, and organizations.

Idea: Individuals, Organizations, and Institutions Are Inherently Paradoxical

If so many things can be described in oxymoronic ways, there must also be a great deal of ambiguity in our organizations and institutions.

Creative Thinking Skills to Be Developed: Looking from a Different Perspective; Being Original

To be honest, the activity at the second level is not terribly difficult. It should serve as a warm-up for the third level, where your students are asked to compose their own oxymorons to our prescriptions. Thus, the skill of looking from a different perspective is practiced at the first and second levels, and the skill of thinking originally is practiced at the third level. The second level has a healthy amount of critical thinking, but we're hoping that your students will free themselves to produce eight novel expressions at the last level.

Interestingly enough, several scholars have given the "unity of opposites" a prominent place in their theories about creative thinking. George M. Prince (1970) sees creativity as "an arbitrary harmony, an expected astonishment, a habitual revelation, a familiar surprise, a generous selfishness, an unexpected certainty, a formidable stubbornness, a vital triviality, a disciplined freedom, an intoxicating steadiness, a repeated initiation, a difficult delight, a predictable gamble, an ephemeral solidity, a unifying difference, a demanding satisfier, a miraculous expectation, and accustomed amazement." But maybe he is going too far.

Preparing for the Unit

You might toss an oxymoron at your students—or you might point out one in a newspaper, magazine, or book—as an introduction to this unit. It shouldn't be necessary to spend much time leading into the administering of the unit unless many of your students are unfamiliar with the figure of speech.

Presenting the Unit

The first two levels can be conducted as an oral exercise, but we recommend that your students complete the third level individually. The third level has the potential for launching them into a lively discussion and for propelling them into additional investigations. We expect that some of the descriptions of the institutions and organizations will look familiar to your students. Frankly, the descriptions were written with certain well-known institutions and organizations in mind.

Reference

Prince, G. M. 1970. *The Practice of Creativity.* New York: Harper.

43   These Oxys Aren't for Morons

1
We hear the word *oxymoron* a good deal today. As you probably know, it comes from the Greek words for "sharp" *(oxy)* and "stupid" *(moron)*. The word, then, is what it represents—a contradiction in terms. When an oxymoron is used to describe a mixing of opposites in an understandable way, it conveys the idea of reconciling those opposites. That's how an oxymoron such as "stupid genius" is used. It isn't a mistake that someone made in putting words together but a deliberate effort to say that a person who is awfully smart in one way is also awfully dull in another.

What is your favorite oxymoron?

2
Commentators, columnists, and reporters are fond of labeling as oxymorons the names of political organizations and projects and phrases uttered by politicians. Here are some deliberate attempts at producing an oxymoron. What do they mean?

Organized chaos

Militant pacifist

Kindly despot

Stingy charity

Facing the Issues © 1994 Zephyr Press, Tucson, Arizona

Conventional rebel

Unbiased partisan

Defiantly acquiescent

3 Compose original oxymorons for these people, institutions, and organizations:

A person who is musical but "can't carry a tune in a bucket."

An individual who is socially adept but who makes big blunders at times in dealing with people.

A person who is illiterate in one way but very literate in another way.

An individual who has a sweet disposition but occasionally "flies off the handle."

An organization that is corrupt but still represents law and order.

An institution that preaches love but is horribly bigoted.

An organization that supposedly protects the environment but actually poisons it.

A financial institution that made its favorable reputation by advertising its small size (appealing to the small investor) but has become huge.

=44=
Watching the News

Conducting an Experiment about Learning

Overview of the Unit

"Watching the News" consists of a little experiment in listening to and watching a television news program and some follow-up questions. The most important of the questions is the last one: How can insights gained from the experiment be profitably used by your students in their academic experience? Our goal, then, is to inveigle your students into learning about learning.

Idea: Most Learning Takes Place Outside the School Setting

The idea that most learning occurs not at the direction of a teacher but as a result of interactions with the nonacademic world is irrefutable and should be obvious to your students.

Creative Thinking Skill to Be Developed: Putting Ideas into Context

If your students actually do obtain some insights about how people get and process information, it will be interesting to find out how they think these insights can be applied to their own educations. You will want to pick up on their ideas, and so a general discussion of the unit will permit you to do so when all your students have finished "Watching the News."

Preparing for and Presenting the Unit

Discussions of television news programs, radio news programs, television viewing (and listening), and learning by means of more than one sense modality are all excellent ways of leading into this unit. In addition, you can set the stage for it by asking your students whether more of their learning takes place inside or outside of school.

Since this unit must be undertaken over a period of at least two days, there will probably be some informal discussing (and maybe cussing) of the unit inside and outside of your classroom. As far as we are concerned, the more conversations that take place (other than during the ten minutes of television viewing and listening in the experiment) the better. In truth, your students are genuine experts when it comes to evaluating television and radio programs. They may also be fairly good educational psychologists. We have just one important piece of advice: don't have your students rush through this unit; give them time to interview and obtain answers to our questions and their own questions.

44 Watching the News

Let's try a little experiment in listening and seeing. All you need to have is a television set to carry on the experiment. You should be alone when you use the television set so that there will be no distractions.

Turn on your set for five minutes of national news at a time when there will be no commercials. Have the *sound off* but leave the picture on for those five minutes. After you have watched for five minutes, write down what you would have liked to have heard in order to get enough information from the stories to understand them fully.

Next, turn the sound back on. Take a seat near your television set and (a) cover up the screen with paper so that you can't see the picture or (b) take a position near the set where you can't see the screen (as when you are facing in the opposite direction from the set). Listen for five minutes. Then write down what you would like to have seen to get sufficient information in order to understand the news stories fully.

Look at your notes. Which situation was better for understanding the news stories—listening but not seeing the screen or watching but not hearing what was being said? Why?

Watching the News *(continued)*

After reflecting upon the findings of your experiment, do you have any suggestions for the producers of newscasts on television? If so, what are they?

Do blind people prefer to *listen* to the news on radio rather than on television? (If you don't know, find out.) _____ Do deaf people who don't receive closed captioned telecasts bother to *watch* a television set? (Again, if you don't know, find out.) _____ Would being able to read lips help a deaf person? (If you can't answer, try to find out.) _____ If you have any insights about how people get information as a result of your experiment, how can you take advantage of them in your own educational career?

45

Make It Fit, If You Can

Finding Good Jobs for Individuals Looking for Work

Overview of the Unit

We intend to make vocational counselors of your students in this unit in order that they become a little more knowledgeable about the current job market. We also hope to get them a little more psychologically prepared for their roles in the "world of work."

The unit is comprised of an introduction in which we make an obvious observation, namely, people often work at jobs for which they are ill suited, and three little case histories of individuals who are either just entering the job market or who have been unsuccessful in finding the right job. Your students are asked to find jobs for the individuals in three different fields.

Idea: There Is a "Right" Job for Everyone

This idea is idealistic and subject to challenge (as are most of the ideas presented in this book). Throw it out at some point during the progress of the unit.

Creative Thinking Skills to Be Developed: Combining Ideas and Elements; Seeing Relationships; Anticipating Consequences

The combining of ideas and elements called for in this unit is the kind that most of us wouldn't associate with creative thinking, that is, matching people to jobs. But there can be a high degree of creativity in seeing relationships and anticipating consequences when anyone attempts to find the correct job for himself or herself or someone else. Most people who work as personnel officers or vocational counselors would agree. In addition, we suggest that your students invent a job for the three individuals if there isn't one in existence now. It should be quite interesting for you to note how many of your students do imagine jobs that have yet to be created.

Preparing for and Presenting the Unit

In our opinion, almost any time during the school year, and any year from the sixth grade through the twelfth grade, is a good time to present this unit. It calls for more information than your students will have, however. Ideally, they should do some investigating in the fields of municipal government, the travel industry, and the newspaper business. That kind of research is best accomplished by means of interviews, but there are many sources in libraries that can give your students clues about possible "ideal" jobs for the three individuals described in the unit. Although a student may not be interested in the fields mentioned, he or she could possibly pick up some useful information and also be able to transfer some of his or her findings to other fields.

Since this unit should have your students doing some research in the field or in a library, it should take several days to complete. The unit is not likely to be successful unless your students have time to give it a good deal of thought.

If you find that our three examples of people searching for a good-fitting job are not sufficiently interesting to your students, please replace them with other individuals who would be more appropriate. It is quite possible that your students won't be able to relate to any of the personalities in the unit. On the other hand, we are hoping that the three represent types of people who typically have problems finding the right place for themselves in the working world.

45 Make It Fit, If You Can

Do people get the jobs for which they are suited? In spite of vocational counseling, tests of skills and preferences, and the like, it is an open question as to whether the jobs people get are more a matter of circumstances (availability of certain kinds of jobs, geographical location, and so on) or of inclination and ability. If someone is painfully shy, he or she won't be comfortable in sales or in jobs where it is necessary to be particularly sociable. But "shy" people do become entertainers—or at least some of them tell us they are shy. We can presume that their need for something else overcomes their shyness. Conversely, if someone is very gregarious, he or she won't be happy as a night guard or cooped up in an office where there is almost no one around.

What should be the "fit" for the following people? Choose a job that you know about or one that you can imagine (new jobs are being created all of the time) for these individuals:

A young woman, age twenty-two, has just finished graduating from a small liberal arts college. Her major was architecture history and her minor was French. She was an excellent student all through high school and college. Her hobbies are working on old cars and weaving. The young lady's favorite sports are swimming and tennis. All during high school and college she had only a few close friends.

No jobs are available in museums, where her training would ordinarily take her. She decides to go into the travel industry. In what job would she be happy and successful? Describe the job and tell why she would be good at it.

Make It Fit, If You Can (continued)

A man of thirty-two has had a string of jobs since he graduated from technical high school in a large city. The jobs have all been in the construction trades. In every case but one (when he quit because the job was too boring), he has been let go because he always tells his supervisors that they aren't doing the work efficiently or correctly. (He is usually right.) Now he is taking stock of himself and trying to decide what he'll do with his life. His parents have been supportive—in more ways than one—but they are becoming exasperated with him. Although thirty-two isn't old, he knows that by the time he is forty he'll have an unenviable job record and virtually no assets.

The man decides that he'll go to work for the city and trusts that his talents will be utilized better than they have been in the past. At what job can he do well for the municipal government? Describe it and tell why it will be a good fit for him.

A young man is presently working part-time as a checker in a supermarket. He dropped out of high school after completing the eleventh grade. In high school, his grades were below average, but he did very well in art classes. In fact, he won a citywide contest for young artists by entering a well-conceived collage. Aside from his artistic pursuits, his hobbies are watching television and snorkeling. Now he wants to get married, but he doesn't have a job that will satisfy his fiancee's need for financial security. She is a secretary for an insurance company.

The young man figures that his future is in commercial art as a graphics artist, but because of his lack of experience he can't land a job in that field. Then he decides to try the newspaper business. What job could he do well at in that field? Describe the job and tell why he would be good at it.

Facing the Issues © 1994 Zephyr Press, Tucson, Arizona

46

Mañana **Never Comes (or Does It?)**

Taking a Close Look at Using Time Wisely and at Procrastinating

Overview of the Unit

Your students are reintroduced to the idea of procrastination in the introduction, and then they are asked to put themselves in five situations that
require decisions about managing time. The unit is, therefore, a straight-
forward attempt on our part to cause your students to reflect a little
about the one thing all of us must manage, either consciously or unconsciously, throughout our lives.

Idea: We All Must Attempt to Manage Our Time Wisely

Some of your students should be able to recite the maxim "Procrastination is the thief of time" when you introduce this unit to your class. One
or more may know the adage "If you want to get something done, give it
to a busy person." This last saying is at the heart of the unit.

Creative Thinking Skill to Be Developed: Anticipating Consequences

The planners of the world seem to be the ones who get things done
and reap the rewards of their efforts. Those who put off or act on the
spur of the moment can be lucky sometimes, but their chances of being

rewarded are not as good as those of the planners. The skill of looking ahead and guessing the consequences of actions and events is a wonderful one to develop in young people.

Preparing for the Unit

There are some really obvious times at which this unit can be presented—to indulge in a weak pun, at which times it can be timely. Maybe it would be better to administer it at a less obvious occasion, one that doesn't foreshadow a big assignment or the necessary preparations for an event. You can judge best when, or if, the unit will have its intended effect of causing your students to reflect upon how they are managing their time.

Presenting the Unit

We hope not to be heavy-handed in this treatment of a very familiar theme. Perhaps your "touch" will save us if we have been too preachy. In that vein, the unit probably can best be administered with a somewhat casual approach. No need to overemphasize the message. Let your students come up with natural responses to the five situations that can be followed by action or procrastination. A general discussion of those responses may be quite revealing to you.

Following through with the Unit

For some classes, a follow-up activity, such as cinquain writing, might be productive. Single concepts such as time, hope, spring, friends, fish, truth, cats, and so on, lend themselves to the cinquain format. You can teach the "legitimate" cinquain of originator Adelaide Crapsey, with its syllabic pattern of 2-4-6-8-2 for the five lines, or the modified version that features 1-2-3-4-1 word for each line. If you don't have an example of a cinquain handy, here is an attempt at each form:

Raindrops	(2 syllables, stating the subject)
Liquid sunshine	(4 syllables, describing the subject)
Falling and splattering	(6 syllables of action)
Makes me miserable and sad	(8 syllables, expressing a feeling)
I'm drenched!	(2 syllables, restating the subject)

Rain	(one word, the subject of the poem)
Damp, cold	(two words, describing the subject)
Pouring down hard	(three words of action)
Makes me feel depressed—	(four words, expressing feelings)
Wet!	(another word for the subject)

Note: Punctuation is at the discretion of the versifier.

46 *Mañana* **Never Comes (or Does It?)**

The most precious "commodity" in our lives is time. Without it, obviously nothing else means anything—or even exists. Some people, unfortunately, become adept at wasting time. They spend it as if it were a limitless resource. When you are young, time seems inexhaustible. There's always tomorrow . . . and the day after . . . or next year. People who put off doing tasks are called procrastinators, as you probably know. "Procrastination is the thief of time" is an old saying that will never go out of favor. There will always be people who put off what they know they should do now.

Are we justified in putting off anything? Maybe it's a good idea sometimes not to act rashly, to "sleep on it." Here are some situations that can either be acted upon very soon or postponed. Tell how you would react to each and explain why.

Almost everyone has bought tickets for the rock concert that will be held in three weeks in the civic auditorium. Since the seating is limited, there is every chance that the concert will sell out. What should you do?

You know that your six-months checkup at the dentist was supposed to take place more than a month ago. The receptionist must have missed your name when she was supposed to phone and remind you. Since seeing the dentist is extremely disagreeable to you, you are just as pleased to wait until someone discovers the oversight. Should you wait until the next checkup is due? Why or why not?

You learn of the death of a good friend's father. It happened yesterday. You feel that you must express your condolences to your friend, but you don't know when you should speak or write to your friend. When should you act?

Facing the Issues © 1994 Zephyr Press, Tucson, Arizona

One of your teachers is fond of giving huge assignments. Each year the teacher specifies that a long report (with bibliography, footnotes, and so on) must be turned in a week before the end of the term. No late papers will be accepted. There is plenty of time to do the report since it is assigned at the beginning of the term. You guess that a week of frantic effort (or maybe even three days) would be sufficient to complete the assignment before the deadline. The teacher advises working on it throughout the term because certain resources may be in short supply toward the end of the term. What is your plan for completing the report?

You are really steamed at your best friend, who, according to another friend, made a nasty remark about you. When should you act, or should you?

47

Perfection

Exploring the Idea of Striving for Perfection

Overview of the Unit

"Perfection" is a fairly complex unit. It starts off with three quotations by individuals who are disappointed in the results of their efforts. A series of questions about the three persons follows. Your students are then asked to bestow each of the disappointed people with seven attributes. Thereupon we ask if having contributed to making personalities of The Old Timer, Faye, and Nigel has changed their minds about which one would be most likely to be satisfied at the end of his or her efforts. Finally, we ask your students to assess themselves with regard to the urge to do things just right.

Idea: Striving for Perfection Can Be a Frustrating Business

Perfectionists, by definition, are never really satisfied. How many people who call themselves perfectionists really are? Many are just "fussbudgets."

Creative Thinking Skill to Be Developed: Elaborating

This unit explores one aspect of human nature rather deeply. Therefore, the emphasis is more upon reflecting and probing than upon original thinking, although the skill of elaborating is called for in filling out the characteristics of the disappointed trio. In general, however, your students are required to think seriously when responding to the questions. In contrast to many of the units in this book, there isn't much of the whimsical about it.

Preparing for the Unit

Since this isn't a lighthearted unit, it would probably be wise to pick a time for presenting it when your students are in a rather sober mood. (Sober, not somber.) At least, we don't foresee very much humor coming out of their engaging in the unit, albeit there might very well be some amusing personalities created for Nigel, Faye, and The Old Timer.

Presenting the Unit

You may have other ideas for "Perfection," but we see it as a unit that will be most successful if it is undertaken individually by your students. As usual, a discussion at its completion should prove profitable in terms of exchanging ideas and opening minds, but it is the kind of exercise that can best be experienced, step by step, by the student puzzling over the questions alone.

47 Perfection

"Drat it!" the old timer exclaimed. "That's number 274. I never seem to get it right. The horseradish was just a bit too dominant."

"Rats!" Faye shouted. And then she shouted again. "It's never the way I want it to be. It just doesn't hang right in back."

"Horrible effect, I'm afraid," murmured Nigel. "We failed to get the lighting correct in that scene. It will never do at all."

1 The three statements of dissatisfaction, each one about something that didn't go right, were uttered by people engaged in different projects, but their work has something in common—it depends upon inspiration and hard work to be successful. Perhaps their work, as it was when they spoke, would seem quite satisfactory to others, but each of these people saw a serious flaw in what he or she did.

Answer the following questions:

The first speaker is a _____. He was trying to create _____. The second speaker is a _____. She was dissatisfied with _____. The third speaker is a _____. He is involved in _____.

2 Will any of those three people ever be completely satisfied with the product they create? Which one of the three is most likely to come closest to getting the exact result he or she wants? _____

Why did you choose that person?

Facing the Issues © 1994 Zephyr Press, Tucson, Arizona

Take the three people and give each of them all of these:

A full name

An age

A nationality

A family

An educational background

A professional or vocational background

A favorite food

The "Drat it!" man   The "Rats!" woman   The "Horrible effect" man

Now, consider the question above again: which one of the three individuals is most likely to be satisfied when she or he stops working on his or her project? Have you changed your mind? If so, why?

3 Have you ever thought you had something done just about right, and then discovered it wasn't really right? No one could tell you it was right because you knew it wasn't the way it should be. What was it you were doing that didn't come out just right?

Being satisfied with what you have done is important. A sense of accomplishment is one of the best feelings anyone can have. But many people seem never to be satisfied with what they do. Others are too easily satisfied with their efforts, often to the regret of people who come into contact with their work. Where would you place yourself on that scale? Are you nearer to the perfectionist or to the easily satisfied person?

What is the price the perfectionist must pay for being that way?

What is the price the too-easily-satisfied person pays? Or does she or he pay a price at all?

═════════**48**═════════

Fifty Is Way Too Many

Examining Some Surpluses

Overview of the Unit

This unit begins with the familiar trip to the store. (Perhaps mall would be a more up-to-date word.) The student is to buy an assortment of items that someone needs or wants. When the student comes home and leaves the sack of items purchased in the hall closet, a little brother looks at them and speculates about how they might be used. The unit ends with questions about those items, since there is a surfeit of each, and how the student might dispose of them.

Idea: Overconsumption, Waste, and Inefficiency Are Problems in Contemporary Society

Although conspicuous consumption is somewhat out of fashion, we still have enormous problems with waste in our society.

Creative Thinking Skill to Be Developed: Combining Ideas and Elements

The creative thinking skill is called for in the middle of the unit, not at the end. The student is to try to figure out how the diverse items in the sack can be used at the same time. Some ingenious and perhaps hilarious responses might come forth from your students.

Preparing for the Unit and Presenting It

A few of the items described in the unit could actually be on display in your classroom if you make the first part of the unit an oral activity. You may actually possess candy bars, gum, a ski jacket, socks, and a thermometer. The pencils should be readily available in your classroom. It helps to have the actual objects on display in cases where young people have to imagine ways of combining and using them. Having a chance to see or touch objects, even though they are very common ones, allows your students to think of the problem in this unit as a realistic one.

The unit ends with your students being asked what they might do if they had too many of the six items. Although this part doesn't make your students think in an especially creative way, it is an opportunity for them to think a little more widely and deeply about how we use and dispose of our material goods. You can hope that one or more of your students will think of altruistic solutions to the problem.

48 Fifty Is Way Too many

1 Let's say you are planning to go to the store today to buy a variety of things. You want to get some candy and gum. How many candy bars will you buy? _____ How much gum will you buy? _____ You are going to a ski resort over the weekend, but your jacket is worn out. How many ski jackets should you take with you? _____ At the moment you don't have any pencils and you are going to have a math exam tomorrow. How many pencils should you buy? _____ You find that all of your athletic socks have holes, and you are going to play tennis tomorrow afternoon. How many pairs of socks should you purchase? _____ You also decide to buy a thermometer to replace your mother's, which you broke last week.

2 All of your purchases end up in one sack because you went to one of the "one-stop" stores that sells all kinds of things, from groceries to hardware. You put them in the hall closet when you come home, and then your little brother happens to see them. When he looks inside the big sack, he figures that someone is going to use them all at the same time.

Your brother likes to count, and so he counts everything in the sack. There are

_____ pieces of gum
_____ candy bars
_____ ski jacket(s)
_____ pencils
_____ pairs of socks
one thermometer

Your brother is puzzled. He can't imagine why anyone would want all of those things right now—or whenever they all will be used. He gets an idea. Yes, he is sure what someone will do with the gum, candy, jacket(s), pencils, socks, and thermometer all at once.

What activity does your brother have in mind?

3 Besides trying to sell these items, what would you do if

you won a case of fifty candy bars at a raffle?

you had a box of ten pencils at school and needed only two?

you were given two identical ski jackets for Christmas?

you were to buy a big pack of gum and then your dentist told you that *none* of those pieces of gum should ever enter your mouth?

Facing the Issues © 1994 Zephyr Press, Tucson, Arizona

someone gave you an extra thermometer?

you were to receive five pairs of socks for your birthday, all of which were too big?

=====49=====

Squeaks, Pops, and Smells

Recalling Sensory Experiences and Making Visual Representations of Voices

Overview of the Unit

The unit starts out by quizzing your students about their powers of observation. It then queries them about the sounds telephones make and the voices of people who talk on the telephone. It finishes with an invitation to make visual representations of three voices that they can recognize on the telephone. This unit represents a departure from the majority of units in *Facing the Issues* because it culminates in a drawing activity. In a classroom world that is dominated by words, some young people can feel defeated. For various reasons, including relative unfamiliarity with English, shyness, speaking and hearing problems, and learning disabilities, these young people feel more comfortable in nonverbal activities for genuine intellectual growth. However, this unit is essentially challenging, and it may not at first appeal to young people, even those who are more comfortable in activities that don't require writing or speaking. It requires several kinds of thinking, and representing voices in line and color isn't an easy task.

Idea: People Have Quite Distinctive Voices, and These Can Be Represented Visually

Many people, including receptionists and secretaries, instantly recognize the telephone voices of people they deal with on a regular basis. The voice, of course, can be given a visual representation by means of various electronic devices such as the oscilloscope.

Creative Thinking Skills to Be Developed:
Being Sensitive and Aware; Being Original

In addition to being sensitive and aware with regard to the phenomena mentioned in the first two sections of the unit, your students are asked to do some remembering. The mental faculty of memory is basic to all intellectual activity. It can't be overlooked as an important component of creative thinking.

We have a hunch that younger children are somewhat more aware of the little events around them than are older youngsters, but we have no data to support that belief. The first part of this unit will provide you with an opportunity to test our hypothesis. You can compare your students' responses with those of younger children you know. Do your students remember the last time they saw a lavender garment? (We're not sure we do!)

Preparing for the Unit

By asking one or two questions about the little ordinary events happening around the school or in the community, you can warm up your students for this unit. For example, you might ask a question about how the front doors of the school are locked. That kind of question would be most appropriate if there has been any break-in at the school in the past year. Or you might ask one of your students to describe the shrubs immediately outside the classroom (if there are any)—without looking out of the window. Any questions concerning all-too-familiar natural objects would be ideal for leading into the unit.

Presenting the Unit

We might make a case that your students should do this unit individually. There isn't much need to have a class discussion concerning their remembrances of events such as the last time they heard a brake squeak or smelled a piece of burnt toast. Whatever you plan during and following the administration of the unit should be low key, especially with regard to the individual student's renditions of voices on the telephone. This unit is really one that you can just briefly introduce and then let what will happen happen.

49 Squeaks, Pops, and Smells

1 Let's see how observant you are. When was the first time you heard a brake squeak?

Where were you?

When was the last time you saw a bubble pop?

What were you doing when the bubble popped?

When was the last time you saw someone wearing a garment that was colored lavender?

What was the garment?

Describe the person who was wearing it.

When was the last time you smelled burnt toast?

Who burned it?

2 Let's go a little farther with the game. Do all of the doors in the place where you live open in the same way? How do they open?

Are both sides of your face identical? If not, how do they differ?

Facing the Issues © 1994 Zephyr Press, Tucson, Arizona

Squeaks, Pops, and Smells (continued)

How many different ways have you heard telephones ring? Take a moment and imagine them in your "mind's ear." Now describe them.

3 Some people remember voices as well as, or better than, they remember faces. Can you recognize the voices of friends and relatives on the telephone? Name two or three voices that you always recognize on the telephone.

Voice 1 _____

Voice 2 _____

Voice 3 _____

Now think about those voices, but not about the people—just their voices. If you have a box of crayons or some colored pens or pencils, draw designs using the colors that fit those voices. The voices can be any designs you want. A person with a certain kind of voice might make you think of roundness or squiggles or heavy lines. Both the design and the colors should represent the feelings you get when you hear the voices.

Squeaks, Pops, and Smells (continued)

You can use the following space to sketch out your ideas in pencil, and then you can use colors for your final designs.

50
To Have and to Hold

Applying the Concept of Preservation to an Institution or Custom

Overview of the Unit

The concept discussed in this unit is preservation. It is a very ordinary and useful concept, not especially intellectual or voguish. After being given a brief introduction to preservation, your students are asked how fifteen items can be preserved. The items range from the concrete (strawberries) to the abstract (the status quo). A number of other questions are asked about the preservation process, and then your students are invited to write an essay about the wisdom or futility of preserving an institution or custom.

Idea: There Are Institutions that Should Be Preserved, and There Are Others That Should Not Be

We want to hang on to what is good and get rid of what is harmful in every phase of modern life. The question you should ask to follow the unit is, "Which institutions are bad or have outlived their usefulness in our society?"

Creative Thinking Skill to Be Developed: Looking from a Different Perspective

"To Have and to Hold" begins with a good deal of critical thinking, calling upon your students to reflect upon how a variety of items can or cannot be preserved. The mental operations of remembering, analyzing, comparing, and judging are all involved in this activity. Creative thinking is required only in the final section, in which your students are asked to look at a custom or an institution from an unusual point of view for them, namely, from the point of view of whether or not it should be preserved.

Nancy Margulies gives an excellent explanation of how creative and critical thinking work together in *Mapping Inner Space* (1990, 64–65). We believe the functions of the left and right hemispheres of the brain are compatible. It is only when teachers and others evaluate performance prematurely that critical thinking interferes with creative thinking.

Preparing for and Presenting the Unit

Preservation as à concept can crop up in a social studies lesson about maintaining amicable relations between nations or about preserving the Union during the Civil War. It is basic to notions of stability in government, of course, and discussions of anarchy, reform, corruption, and so on, have preservation as a basic concept. Accordingly, there are many times when the unit can be used effectively in helping your students gain understandings of various issues.

Since the unit leads your students to a serious writing activity, one that calls for some research and a good deal of reflection, "To Have and to Hold" should be administered over a period of two or three days. As is typical of these units, your students are given a very wide choice of subjects to investigate. Any established custom or institution should prove to be appropriate for their essays.

Some Words about Essays

Because there is quite a bit to "To Have and to Hold," we have not included a section on the writing of essays. If we had, this would be approximately what we'd say:

> An essay is a piece of writing about a particular subject and can be *from a particular point of view.* It can be used to persuade or convince someone and hence is potentially an argument. For example, the writer may want to convince people that something should be changed or that it should remain the way it is; he or she may want to complain about something; or the essayist may want to praise something.

Before writing an essay, the writer should plan what he or she is going to say. The essay may have a theme or central idea, and this theme will help the writer to organize the points he or she wishes to make in the essay. If the essay is to be about the President as a leader, for instance, the controlling idea is leadership. The writer can then select several aspects of a president's career as a leader; that is, the writer can discuss the president as a leader of a political party, of a nation, and of the world. The writer would emphasize the president's qualities of leadership and accomplishments with respect to various aspects of that person's career.

The arrangement of the different parts of the essay is crucial to its success. The manner in which it is introduced is very important. The writer may decide to begin the essay with an interesting anecdote or a quotation in order to persuade the reader to go on reading the essay.

Finally, the writer may choose to sum up his or her argument succinctly by hitting those points again that seem to the writer to be most important and convincing. Some readers skip down to the final paragraph or two of an essay for the summing up, and so this part is strategically almost as important as the beginning.

Reference

Margulies, Nancy. 1991. *Mapping Inner Space: Learning and Teaching Mind Mapping.* Tucson, Ariz.: Zephyr Press.

50 To Have and to Hold

1
We preserve things in many different ways. In order to keep fish fresh, we use ice. By bronzing baby shoes, many people keep their children's shoes in the same condition that they were when the shoes were outgrown. When we want to preserve something nowadays, we may encase it in plastic. In this exercise, you will be asked to think of how a variety of things might be preserved—that is, how they might be kept, maintained, retained, or sustained.

How would you preserve

strawberries?

the flavor of mint?

the fragrance of roses?

the fragrance of grass after it is mowed?

Facing the Issues © 1994 Zephyr Press, Tucson, Arizona

the color of daffodils?

autumn leaves?

the excitement of a victory?

the sky at daybreak?

an advantage over someone?

dignity?

authority?

youth?

a friendship?

territorial boundaries?

the status quo?

Is there anything you would particularly like to see preserved?

2 Which of the items above would you most like to preserve or have preserved for you? Why?

Would it really be the same if you tried to keep it just as it is? Why or why not?

Is there anything that actually never changes? Why or why not?
What is the difference between conserving something and preserving it?

3 Why don't you write a persuasive essay about the wisdom or futility of preserving a human institution or custom? Choose a subject that you are particularly interested in, and do some research in order to be sure of your ground and also to obtain new information that will make your essay more interesting and persuasive. Jot down the ideas for your essay in the space below.

51

Civic Match-ups

Associating Words about Government

Overview of the Unit

This exercise is the kind that can be used at any time of the year for a review or a gamelike activity. We don't recommend it as a test because there are usually several possible answers to any set of three words, which makes scoring difficult, and also because it really works better as an informal activity. In the unit, we present seven sets of three words each and ask your students what words can "go" with the sets. In other contexts, this is a word association game or test. After completing the exercise, your students are asked to create an exercise of their own.

Idea: There Are Certain Words
That We Commonly Associate with Others

We use trite expressions in describing the political scene, and so your students shouldn't have too much difficulty in identifying them in this exercise.

Creative Thinking Skill to Be Developed: Seeing Relationships

This activity is entirely concerned with associating, that is, with seeing relationships. Because we all don't make the same kind of associations, a number of psychological tests have been devised to give hints as to the personalities of the individuals who take the tests.

If we were to make this into a test of creative thinking, one of the abilities that might be measured would be originality. Those students who can come up with out-of-the-ordinary responses can be considered to be original thinkers. We also could ask for more than one response to a set of three words, and that would give us measures of fluency and flexibility. If you are interested, you might try either variation of this activity. To try the first variation, all you need to do is to change the instructions to "Can you think of a word that goes with these three words that very few people would think of?" For the second variation, you can just ask for as many responses to each set of words as your students can think of within a reasonable period of time.

Preparing for the Unit

The only advice we have to offer concerning this unit is that you let your students know before they tackle it that it is not a test. The unit should be regarded as more of a word game. Some of your students are probably good at word games, and some probably don't care for them (and consequently are not very good at them). You should make it clear that the unit is for fun, thus taking the pressure off those who struggle with this kind of activity.

Presenting the Unit

We definitely had in mind seven words that went with the seven sets:

federal	budget	fiscal	*deficit*
market	standard	bullion	*gold*
campaign	bills	political	*reform*
herring	tape	ink	*red*
bottom	reception	item	*line*
living	buster	oil	*trust*
CIA	industrial	international	*espionage*

As we say in the unit, there certainly can be other answers. For example, "finance" might go with "campaign," "bills," and "political." At this writing, "reform" is more in the news. We encourage you to substitute items for the ones given in the unit if you see an opportunity to put over certain points or review subject matter covered in class.

The last section, in which your students are encouraged to make their own exercise, can be something that they can share with each other when they have finished the unit. You might compile a dozen or so of the best items and submit them to the entire class.

51 Civic Match-ups

In this exercise, you will be given sets of three words. The words all have to do with civics. Your job is to think of a single word that is commonly associated with each of the three words of a set. So you think, "What word commonly goes with the three words given?" The relationship is not always a logical one, and so you have to use your imagination in thinking about what most people would think of when reading or hearing the three words. Here is an example. You are given these words: pay, year, kick. You might think of "off" when you see pay (as in pay-off) and year (off-year election) and kick (a kickoff banquet for a candidate). Or you might not. There are many possible answers.

See what you can do with the seven sets of words that follow.

market	standard	bullion	_____
federal	budget	fiscal	_____
campaign	bills	political	_____
herring	tape	ink	_____
bottom	reception	item	_____
living	buster	oil	_____
CIA	industrial	international	_____

Why don't you try your hand at devising a similar game? Come up with sets of three words that are commonly associated with one word for each set. You can use the space below to work out your ideas.

Facing the Issues © 1994 Zephyr Press, Tucson, Arizona

=52=
The Job Picture

Thinking about Expectations and a Future Job

Overview of the Unit

The final unit of *Facing the Issues* is a forward-looking exercise about expectations. It ends with a request for your students to draw pictures of themselves on their "first" important job. Since the theme of the unit is expectations, there is an introductory section about people who expect too much or too little, and then your students are asked what kinds of expectations they should have in ten situations. This section is followed by questions about gifted athletes and traffic. Finally, there is an invitation to your students to draw themselves in two situations: (1) working at a job, with all of their hopes fulfilled; (2) working in a less-than-ideal situation on that first important job.

Idea: It Should Prove Helpful for Anyone to Visualize Himself or Herself as a Productive Member of Society

A positive, but realistic, self-image for each of your students can be encouraged by exercises such as this one.

Creative Thinking Skill to Be Developed: Visualizing Colorfully and Richly

This unit calls for some drawing as well as writing, which may be a relief for your more inarticulate students. We want all of your students to project themselves into the future by actually getting a picture of themselves at work. Regardless of the individual students and their hoped-for occupation, they all should have images, however vivid or vague, of themselves at work on an "important" job. Without those images, their expectations are most likely pessimistic.

Torrance and Safter (1993) state in *Making the Creative Leap Beyond* that "rich, colorful, and exciting imagery has long been regarded by many scholars as the foundation or mainspring of all creativity." More and more people are recognizing the importance of imagining their performances prior to giving them. Many athletes, in particular, spend a great deal of time seeing their performances in their minds' eyes in great detail before engaging in competition. We think that imagining oneself performing at work is also a particularly important activity for your students.

Preparing for the Unit

A practical consideration for some teachers in preparing for this unit is to make sure students have the equipment for drawing the two sketches at the end of the unit. Other than having extra equipment and materials, you may not have much to do in connection with "The Job Picture." The students should be left to their own devices and thoughts in completing the unit. It is doubtful if even a general discussion of the middle section will add much to their enlightenment, although the part about gifted athletes could bring up some interesting points.

Presenting the Unit

Whereas the theory of "imaging" before performing is that an individual should conjure up mental images of an *ideal* situation in order to be able to carry out optimal behaviors, we have chosen also to ask your students to draw another work situation that lacks one or many important positive elements for them. The justification for having your students draw a picture of themselves in a less-than-ideal situation is that we want them to have their high hopes tempered a little by reality. Rarely is that first job ideal in all respects. In what ways may things be unsatisfactory? We leave that to your students' imaginations.

Reference

Torrance, E. Paul, and Tammy Safter. 1993. *Making the Creative Leap Beyond.* Buffalo, N.Y.: Bearly Limited.

52 The Job Picture

1 Expectations are important. Sometimes, when you expect a lot, you are keenly disappointed, and that can make you angry or depressed. On the other hand, when you don't expect much, and you don't get much, your aspirations can be too low. That is, by not trying to reach certain goals and working hard to attain them, you may be selling yourself short.

There are many people who try not to "get their hopes up" because they are afraid of being disappointed. When a future event is entirely out of their control, that may be a good way for them to be. For example, it is silly for anyone to bank on winning a large lottery prize. People who talk about what they will do with all of their winnings usually know that their dreams won't be realized, but they enjoy the dreaming anyway.

Your expectations determine your behavior to a great extent, and your reactions to the actual events will initially be greatly influenced by your expectations. For instance, during the Olympic Games we often see people, both competitors and spectators, bitterly disappointed when athletes who were heavily favored to win come in second. Sometimes the expectations were unrealistic, and the athletes' performances were really remarkable even though they didn't result in victory. Instead of being joyous, the occasion becomes a near-tragedy—because of expectations.

2 Is it better to have great expectations or small expectations in the following situations? Explain your answers.

When you are going to a big amusement park for the first time.

When you start a book that everyone is raving about.

When you come to school with new clothes on.

After turning in a report you have worked hard on for a week.

After turning in a report you didn't work on so hard but thought you could bluff your way through.

After writing a friend and expecting a reply.

When you have a particular teacher for the first time.

As you participate in or watch your team start to play an important game.

When you invest all of your savings in the stock market.

The first time you drive a car.

The Job Picture *(continued)*

3 When heading out of the city on Friday afternoon, should you expect an easy trip? What should your expectations be?

If you are a talented athlete, should you have high hopes of becoming a professional? Why or why not?

4 Think about your own ambitions for a few minutes. What vocational goals do you have? What do you want your first important job to be like? You may have high hopes for a really good job that you will enjoy. First, briefly describe your first important job, and then draw two pictures of yourself. One picture should show you at work and doing very well in an ideal situation. The other picture should show you on the job in a less-than-ideal situation. It doesn't have to be a bad situation—it's just not nearly as good as you'd like it to be. Color your pictures and put as many details in them as you can think of.

What is your job going to be like?

The Job Picture (continued)

Devote the space below to the two pictures of you at work.

Give your students problem-solving skills to last a lifetime!

WHAT NEXT?
Futuristic Scenarios for Creative Problem Solving
by Robert E. Myers and E. Paul Torrance

Grades 6–12

Tap into students natural interest in the future with writing activities you can incorporate into language arts, social studies, or humanities programs.

Select from 52 exciting units to nourish creative thinking and to inspire thinking about the future. Each unit includes an overview, warm-up topics, suggestions for presentation, and writing exercise.

388 pages, 81/2" x 11", softbound.
ZB49-W $29

TURNING LEARNING INSIDE OUT
A Guide for Using Any Subject to Enrich Life and Creativity
by Herbert L. Leff and Ann Nevin

Grades K–12

Turn learning loose on life by showing students how to take what they learn in academic content areas and apply it to their lives outside the classroom.

Help your students gain a new sense of purpose, excitement, and value for learning. Teach them how to develop awareness plans—cognitive bridges that link academic and real-world problem solving.

Have fun with dozens of "minds-on" activities. Apply flexible strategies to all content areas and educational settings. Your students will—

- Find academic content more involving and relevant
- Combine metacognitive skills and content learning
- Develop a self-directed and cooperative approach to learning

You and your students will discover that these strategies lead to a far-reaching enrichment of overall creativity and enjoyment of life.

256 pages, 8 1/2" x 11", softbound.
ZB48–W . . . $29

CALL, WRITE, OR FAX FOR YOUR FREE CATALOG!

ORDER FORM   ☎ Please include your phone number in case we have questions about your order.

Qty.	Item #	Title	Unit Price	Total
	ZB49-W	What Next?	$29	
	ZB48-W	Turning Learning Inside Out	$29	

Name _____

Address _____

City _____

State _____ Zip _____

Phone (_____) _____

Method of payment (check one):

❏ Check or Money Order   ❏ Visa

❏ MasterCard   ❏ Purchase Order attached

Credit Card No. _____

Expires _____

Signature _____

Subtotal	
Sales Tax (AZ residents, 5%)	
S & H (10% of Subtotal)	
Total (U.S. Funds only)	

CANADA: add 22% for S& H and G.S.T.

100% SATISFACTION GUARANTEE

Upon receiving your order you'll have 90 days of risk-free evaluation. If you are not 100% satisfied, return your order within 90 days for a 100% refund of the purchase price. No questions asked!